Lady Featherlow's Tea Room

PATRINA McKENNA

Copyright © 2021 Patrina McKenna

All rights reserved

This book is a work of fiction. Names, characters, places, and incidents either are products of the author's imagination or are used fictitiously. Any resemblance to actual persons, living or dead, events, or locales is entirely coincidental.

Publisher: Patrina McKenna

patrina.mckenna@outlook.com

ISBN-13: 978-1-8381827-1-7

Also by Patrina McKenna

Romantic comedy with a twist!

Truelove Hills
Truelove Hills – Mystery at Pebble Cove
Truelove Hills – The Matchmaker
Granny Prue's Bucket List
Christmas with the Neighbours
Trouble at Featherlow Forbes Menswear
Lady Featherlow's Tea Room

Feel good fantasy for all the family!

GIANT Gemstones
A Galaxy of Gemstones
The Gemstone Dynasty
Enrico's Journey
Summer Camp at Tadgers Blaney Manor

DEDICATION

For my family and friends

PROLOGUE

The butler at Featherlow Manor opened the study door for Mr Livermore to enter. Annabelle was standing by the window. 'Mr Livermore, what an unexpected pleasure. I must say I am most intrigued after receiving your call yesterday.'

Mr Livermore pointed to the chair behind the desk. 'May I?'

Annabelle nodded as the family solicitor placed his briefcase on the floor and extracted a thin document. 'Please take a seat, Lady Featherlow. You may need one.'

Annabelle sat down with her hands in her lap. This whole situation seemed very surreal; why was Mr Livermore sitting at her husband's desk with a twinkle in his eye?

'As you know, Lady Featherlow, Clara Smith was a much-loved member of the community in Featherlow Bottom. Indeed, we both knew her for, what must it be now?'

Annabelle sighed, 'Thirty-five years from when I recruited her as Freddie's nanny.'

'Ah, yes. I remember drawing up her employment contract at the time. You were very kind to Clara over the years, Lady Featherlow, even to the point of allowing her to reside above the village tea room and run the business as a simple cake shop when your son was no longer in need of her services.'

Annabelle smiled. 'It was a pleasure. "Clara's Cakes" has been at the heart of the village for many years.' Annabelle's smile faded, and she wrung her hands together. 'I have no idea what will happen to the shop now; no-one could replace Clara.'

Mr Livermore took Lady Featherlow's words as the perfect cue. 'Clara had a vision for the future of the shop. She had no family of her own and has left the premises to you in her Last Will and Testament.'

Annabelle gasped. 'But the premises weren't hers to leave to anyone. We own all the land and buildings in Featherlow Bottom. Didn't you remind Clara of that when she made her bequest?'

Mr Livermore lowered his head. 'I didn't like to spoil her excitement. Of course, you are free to do what you like with the shop, but in Clara's eyes she wanted you to undertake some renovation work and re-name it as "Lady Featherlow's Tea Room". She has left all her worldly goods to you; there's just a small amount of furniture and clothing in the apartment above the shop and two thousand, six hundred and eighty-four pounds, nineteen pence, in her bank account. It's all yours now, Lady Featherlow, along with this letter.' Mr Livermore dipped into his briefcase and stood up before handing a sealed envelope to Annabelle. 'I'll be on my way now. You know where I am if you have any queries.'

1

MIDSUMMER'S DAY

Featherlow Bottom was a hive of activity. A fair had come to the village for the midsummer celebrations. There were six coachloads of tourists due by lunchtime. Archie's Alehouse had erected a marquee on the village green to cater for the influx of thirsty revellers and bunting was being tied between the ornate lamp posts lining both sides of the narrow winding river.

Lady Featherlow's Tea Room had spilt out of its luxury two-storey premises onto the embankment. Flowers adorned the wrought iron tables in Lady Featherlow's favourite colour – pink. The ornate footbridge adjacent to the tea room gave easy access to the other side of the river, which would be in the sun all afternoon at this time of year. Pink umbrellas had been erected over there for the convenience of the customers.

Lady Featherlow stood outside the shop with hands on hips admiring the scene. The manager of the tea room stepped outside to join her. 'The sight is magnificent, is it not?'

Annabelle swooned. 'It's breathtaking, Jules.'

'Not as breathtaking as you, Lady Featherlow.'

Lady Featherlow laughed; at thirty-five, Jules was the same age as her son. Still, she'd had such fun over the last few months transforming the tea room and recruiting an expert team, headed up by the very charming Jules Peridot. At over six feet tall, with short black hair, and sparkling green eyes, Jules sent hearts racing. Visitors to the tea room came from far and wide.

Annabelle brushed a fleck from Jules's shoulder. He flinched. 'Am I not perfect?'

Annabelle laughed. 'You're always perfect, Jules. It was just a speck of flour. It's not surprising with all the work going on in the kitchen today. Are you happy with the temporary staff we hired?'

Jules's face dropped. 'I wasn't going to mention it, but two of the waiting staff haven't turned up. It will be a challenge today.'

Annabelle handed Jules her bag. 'Then I must help. Find a safe place for this and fetch me a uniform. I've always wanted to try one on. The designs are exquisite.'

'But Lady Featherlow!'

'No "buts" Jules. I can't desert a sinking ship.'

'We're not sinking yet.'

'Humour me, Jules. I can drop my title for a day. Most of the customers won't have any idea who I am. I'll be an undercover boss.'

Jules gulped. 'Now I'm worried.'

Annabelle playfully slapped his arm. 'I'm sure you have nothing to worry about. Now, come along, there's no time to waste.'

*

Less than an hour later, Annabelle was in her element. Jules was surprised at how easily she had transformed from Lady of the Manor into a gracious and charming waitress. He was full of admiration for his boss, who was proving to be an extremely competent member of the team.

So far, only Mavis Lorne and her niece, Loretta, had recognised Lady Featherlow in her new role. Loretta's mouth fell open when Annabelle placed a plate of scones in front of her and Mavis squealed. 'Lady Featherlow! If I hadn't been here to see it myself, then I never would have guessed you needed a job.'

Annabelle smiled. 'I'm only helping out for the day. Are you both excited about today's events? You've been very wise securing this table outside by the bridge. I've just seen two coaches arrive. We'll be rushed off our feet soon. However, I must admit I'm surprised to see you both. Aren't you opening the shop today?'

Mavis's eyes clouded over. 'There's something I need to tell you. Since the tea room has become so popular, our business has dropped off.'

Annabelle gasped. 'I'm shocked. Your family has run Lorne's Lemonade and Icicles for as long as I can remember. It's an institution – a landmark associated with Featherlow Bottom. Indeed, I remember Freddie raving about your Luscious Lemon Sorbets with whipped cream and chocolate sprinkles.'

'That was a long time ago, Lady Featherlow. I don't have the energy, or the funds, to make business improvements at my age. I'll be seventy-two next month. You'll soon have a vacant shop, and Loretta will need to move away from Featherlow Bottom to find employment.'

Annabelle glanced at Loretta, who looked like she wanted to be anywhere else other than here. She'd always been a quiet woman, who must now be in her early thirties. Annabelle couldn't imagine her surviving in the great outside world. She felt horrified that, in her excitement at resurrecting the tea room, she'd been oblivious to the fact that some residents in Featherlow Bottom were suffering.

Annabelle noticed Jules looking over at her. She wasn't there to chat, she nodded to him by way of acknowledgement and made her way back into the shop. 'I'm sorry about that, Jules. Mavis was keen to update me on something. I'll get straight back to work.'

*

By two o'clock, Annabelle was flagging. Her legs ached, her feet hurt, and she was tired of explaining herself to albeit just a few of the customers. The day-trippers who didn't recognise her were quite demanding, less than polite, and quite frankly didn't deserve to frequent Lady Featherlow's Tea Room. Annabelle noticed Sam Comfrey sitting on his own in an alcove on the first floor, and she sat down next to him.

'Sam! You don't mind if I join you for a minute or two, do you? My feet are killing me.'

Sam shuffled along the pink velvet studded bench. 'Of course, Lady Featherlow. I've been watching you all morning. Why are you putting yourself through this when you own the whole caboodle? It doesn't suit you at all.'

Annabelle could always rely on Sam to provide a reality check. She leant on the table and placed her head in her hands. 'This has been such a bad idea.'

Sam patted her arm. 'There, there. Don't cry. Another ship will sail in the morning.'

Annabelle sat upright. 'What did you say?'

'Another ship will sail in the morning.'

'Why did you say that?'

'Oh, it's just one of my sayings from my Navy days. I was a sailor, you know.'

Annabelle grabbed Sam's hand. 'I know you were a sailor, Sam. We are all so proud of you. We love hearing about your experiences at sea.'

Sam nodded towards Jules, who was serving a customer. 'Well, I must be off now, or we'll both be in trouble. I've outstayed my welcome, and you're about to get the sack. I'll make my way over to Archie's Alehouse; I'll buy you a pint later if you're stuck for something to do.'

Annabelle managed a small laugh. 'You've cheered me up, Sam. I may well take you up on that drink. Today hasn't been a total disaster. I've learnt a few things.'

Sam stood up. 'You did your best, Lady Featherlow. That's all folk can ask.'

On the realisation that Sam had finally left the building, Jules walked over to join Annabelle. 'Well done, Lady Featherlow. We always struggle to shorten that gentleman's visits.'

Annabelle glared at Jules. 'The gentleman's name is Sam. He lives in the boat-house in the woods. It must be frightfully cold for him in there. Sam is welcome to spend as much time in the tea room as he desires.'

Jules nodded as Annabelle removed her white frilled apron and shoved it at him. 'Where did you put my bag? I really should be off now to mingle with the tourists. It's such an important day for Featherlow Bottom.'

Jules watched as Lady Featherlow headed towards the village green. Well, that was him well and truly reprimanded. Why was his boss so concerned about an old sailor? Jules hadn't liked to mention it, but it was June now – not January – the boat-house wouldn't be cold at this time of the year.

2

AN UNWELCOME COMPANION

By five o'clock, the tea room was still full of customers, and Jules was agitated. One of the permanent waitresses, Trixie, chuckled. 'You're your own worst enemy, Mr Peridot. You need to learn from Lady Featherlow. You should loosen up a bit and stop treating the tea room like a military operation. It doesn't matter if we're a bit late closing tonight; it's a special day. I'll be going straight over to the fair,' Trixie glanced up at her boss, 'and I'm taking you with me.'

*

It was seven-thirty before Trixie found two spare stools in the Archie's Alehouse marquee. 'Take a seat, Mr Peridot, I'll get the beers in.'

Jules sat down opposite Sam, whose beer glass was empty. Jules suspected Sam had been sitting there all afternoon taking up the space of more worthy customers; just like he did in the tea room.

'Jules! You're a sight for sore eyes. I didn't expect you to let your hair down with the likes of us. I guess Trixie dragged you along.'

Jules leant forward. 'It's not *really* cold in your boathouse, is it? Lady Featherlow is concerned for you.'

Sam blushed. 'I don't know where she got that idea from. I'm always nice and toasty back home.'

Jules smirked. He knew Sam was just a loser on the lookout for sympathy and a free drink. He should keep himself to himself instead of making the place look untidy. Jules bore his gaze into the side of the older man's head until Sam stood up and made his way out of the marquee. That was a result.

Trixie returned with three pints. 'Where's Sam gone? I bought him a drink.'

Jules shrugged and took a sip of his pint. 'No idea. He was here one minute; gone the next.'

The nasty streak of the Tea Room Manager hadn't gone unnoticed. Loretta had been watching him make Sam so uncomfortable he was forced to leave. She always kept an eye out for Sam; he was like a father to her. She'd had her suspicions about Jules Peridot from when he'd first set foot in Featherlow Bottom. Loretta may be a woman of few words, but her instinct was spot on. A lot was to be gained from just watching and listening.

Lord and Lady Featherlow were taking a ride on the Ferris wheel. They never missed an opportunity to survey their land from a great height whenever the fair came to the village. On this occasion, however, Annabelle was agitated.

'I'm concerned for some of the residents, Winston. Mavis Lorne advised me today that their business is going under because of what I've done with the tea room. I don't understand why. I know we offer soft drinks in our shop, but we don't cater for ice-creams.'

Winston raised an eyebrow. 'That's not what I heard. Archie told me only last week that the knickerbocker glory he'd tasted in your tea room was top notch. Jules, whatever-his-name, is bringing class to the village. You did well to hire him.'

Annabelle gasped. 'Did you see that?'

'What?'

'There's tarpaulin on the roof of the boat-house, and the windows are boarded up.'

Winston leant across his wife. 'That place needs knocking down. It's nothing more than a shack. We'll get rid of it when Sam passes.'

Annabelle slapped her husband's leg. 'That's not the attitude, Winston. We need to help Sam now! As soon as we get off this wheel, we'll go to see him.'

*

Sam opened the door of the boat-house and turned a bright shade of crimson at the sight of Lord and Lady Featherlow standing before him. 'What a surprise! I'm afraid I can't invite you in.'

Annabelle sensed no good. 'Well, we are coming in, Sam. Why didn't you let us know that your property needed some repairs?'

Sam stood back for the couple to enter. 'It was all my fault; Loretta bought me an oil lamp last Christmas, and I forgot to turn it out. I've made the necessary repairs. This will do me to the end of my days.'

Tears sprang to Annabelle's eyes at the sparsity of Sam's abode. The smoke-stained walls and furniture made her heart sink; it was amazing that Sam was still alive after living in the chargrilled remains of his boat-house since Christmas.

Annabelle linked arms with her husband in a show of solidarity – she wasn't going to let Winston have any say in this. 'We are here to help. We'll wait while you pack a few things then you must come to the manor with us. We have plenty of spare rooms. You will be our guest until we have built you a new home.'

*

Loretta lurked behind a tree. She watched as Sam trudged behind Lord and Lady Featherlow carrying a black plastic sack. Her heart leapt. Finally! Sam was getting some help. She looked down at the box she was holding, Sam wouldn't need his weekly provisions for a while. Loretta now had a problem with what to do with the bread, cheese, ham, and fruit. If she put it in the kitchen in the apartment she shared with her aunt, it would raise suspicion.

'What are you doing out here with all that food?'

Loretta jumped at the sight of Jules Peridot standing behind her. 'I'm having a picnic.'

Jules frowned. 'It isn't safe for you to be here alone in the woods at nine-thirty in the evening. Are you sure you're having a picnic?'

Loretta couldn't stand that man. His sparkling green eyes were twinkling brighter than ever, no doubt due to the effect of a few pints. Loretta sat down on the grass and tore at the loaf of bread, then broke off a lump of cheese and bit into it.

Jules gestured to the grass beside her. 'May I?' Loretta ignored him and kept chewing. Jules sat down next to her. 'You are a woman of few words.'

Loretta shoved the box closer to her unwelcome companion, and he tore at the bread too. Before long he was tucking into the impromptu feast. The couple sat in silence as the sky darkened, bringing a sliver of moon and a dusting of stars. Loretta kept an eye on her watch. It was approaching ten o'clock. She needed to make a run for it; Aunt Mavis would be getting worried; at least she didn't need to take the food home now.

Without a word, Loretta stood up, brushed her skirt down and headed off, leaving her unwelcome companion speechless.

3

TIME FOR A REVIEW

Jules was surprised to receive the call from Lady Featherlow. He checked his appearance in the mirror on his office wall – no specks of flour today. He wanted to look his best when his boss arrived at eleven o'clock for an unscheduled review meeting.

Annabelle sat across the desk from her wayward employee. She unfolded her arms; that stance was an easy giveaway she was annoyed with him. 'Why do we have knickerbocker glories on the menu in the tea room?'

Jules smiled, flashing his perfect white teeth. 'It is good to expand our offering, is it not?'

Annabelle tapped her foot. 'When I interviewed you, I made it clear the tea room should remain authentic. Knickerbocker glories are not in keeping with what we're about.'

Jules chanced his luck. 'I beg to differ, Lady Featherlow. If the demand is there, we should give the customers what they want.'

Annabelle straightened her back. 'We are not just a tea room; we are part of the jigsaw of Featherlow Bottom as a whole. For generations, my husband's family has strived to maintain harmony within the village. Indeed, Featherlow Bottom has won many awards in the "Best Place to Live" category on our local council's website.' What was really bothering Annabelle sprang to the surface, 'I have to say I was particularly disappointed yesterday with the way you spoke about Sam.'

The smile dropped from Jules's face, and Annabelle expected this peacock of a man to throw in the towel. He belonged in a London wine bar, not a village tea room. She'd been blindsided by his charm when she'd recruited him.

Jules leant forward on the desk. 'I don't know what to say.' He was thinking quickly. He had to keep this job – none other would do. He'd been waiting for the tea room to open for months. He continued, 'I'm sorry I misjudged things. Just tell me what you need me to do, and I'll make the necessary changes.'

Annabelle was shocked that the peacock so willingly shed his feathers. She was still annoyed with Jules, though, and took the opportunity to push his ego down through the floor. 'Firstly, I want you to remove any competition with Lorne's Lemonade and Icicles. Secondly, I would like you to spend time with Mavis and Loretta to offer your business and creative skills. I want their shop to be as popular as the tea room.'

Jules nodded, and Annabelle chanced her arm even further. 'I notice from your CV you studied architecture. Why didn't you pursue a career in that field?'

'I mentioned at my interview it was obvious I was more suited to a catering environment.'

Annabelle coughed. 'Oh, yes. I remember now. Well, you would be doing me a big favour if you put your creative and architectural knowledge to work and produced some designs for a boat-house. How long do you think that would take?'

Jules's heart leapt; his suppressed desires were brought to the fore. 'I have a design package on my laptop I can use. It should take me less than a week – I'll work in the evenings.'

Annabelle's frostiness was beginning to thaw. 'That's very good of you. I suggest you focus on the boat-house as a priority. I have a demolition team coming in tomorrow to remove Sam's derelict dwelling. You need to take into account the house will be situated in the woods next to the river, it should be in keeping with the surrounding area and suitable for Sam. Single-storey will be best.'

Jules couldn't believe his luck. He'd kept the job of his curved-ball destiny and had been given an opportunity to do the job of his dreams.

Annabelle stood up. 'Shall we meet again this time next week? I'll bring Sam with me to approve the designs.'

Jules stood up too. 'That will be perfect, Lady Featherlow. I look forward to seeing you both then.'

*

One week later, a newly suited and booted Sam sat next to Lady Featherlow in Jules Peridot's office. Jules breezed in with a tray of tea and doughnuts. 'I brought your favourites, Sam. Wow! I must say you are looking very well.'

Sam brushed the lapel of his jacket. 'Lady Featherlow took me shopping. It's as good a time as any to spend my savings. I hear you're designing me a new house.'

Jules turned his laptop around and sat next to Sam. 'I hope you like my design. I've allowed for two bedrooms, a kitchen-diner, lounge with an open fireplace and a wet room.'

Sam rubbed his chin. 'A wet room? What's one of those?'

Jules blushed. 'I thought it would be more convenient for you than an old-fashioned bathroom. It's a modern way of having a shower.' Jules held his breath.

Sam winked at him. 'It was a nightmare getting in and out of that bath with my old legs. I like your thinking; it's good to be modern.'

Annabelle gave Jules an approving glance. Sam was engrossed in the plans. 'I like the portholes for windows. What's that boat doing outside? The river's not wide enough for a boat.'

Jules's eyes twinkled. 'It's for you to see from your lounge window. You can fill it with plants if you like. I just thought it made a nice touch.'

Annabelle saw a new side to the former peacock. In his "design" mode, he was a different person. She sat quietly to allow the two men time to mull over the plans.

Sam stared at Jules. 'So, when will I be moving into my new home?'

Jules raised his eyebrows at Annabelle, who took Sam's comment as his approval for the work to be carried out. She smiled at Jules and touched Sam's arm. 'I'll get the builders on the case tomorrow. I can assure you there will be no expense spared to ensure you move into your new property as soon as possible.'

Sam blushed. 'Am I that bad a guest at the manor house?'

Annabelle laughed. 'Not at all! We love having you there.' Annabelle turned to face Jules. 'Good work! Now you must turn your attention to Mavis and Loretta. I trust you to work your magic on your next project.'

4

UNWILLING PARTICIPANTS

The following morning, Jules walked into Lorne's Lemonade and Icicles. He'd already noticed the rusty sign outside and the sparse window display. Mavis stood up from a stool behind the counter. 'What can I do you for?'

Jules cringed at the deliberate twist of words to make him feel ill at ease. He sensed this would not be an easy conversation. 'Nothing at the moment. I am here to help.'

Mavis narrowed her eyes. 'We don't need help. We're on our way out of this measly place. If that Annabelle Featherlow has sent you, then she shouldn't have bothered. I'm about to sue her for allowing our business to fall into neglect.'

Jules took a step backwards. 'Is Loretta here?'

'She's gone to the market.'

'Oh, I see. Well, I'd best be on my way then.'

Jules closed the shop door behind him and took in a deep breath. That wasn't at all what he'd expected. Out of the corner of his eye, Jules spotted Loretta cleaning the tables outside Archie's Alehouse. He walked over to speak to her.

Loretta jumped at the sight of Jules. 'Please don't mention to my aunt that you've seen me here.'

Jules took hold of Loretta's hand and guided her to a bench. 'Sit down with me and tell me what's going on.'

Loretta's wild eyes scanned the vicinity. 'I can't. Just go away and leave us alone. If you say anything to Lady Featherlow, then my life is over.' Loretta dashed behind the building, and Jules was left with a more significant predicament than he already had. Not only was he leading a double life, but Loretta was too.

With a heavy heart, Jules returned to the tea room. He needed time to work his way through this nightmare. Jules had to stay focused. If he just got on with his day job, then everything else would fall into place. Trixie was holding the fort while he'd been to see Mavis, she was surprised to see him back so soon. 'That was quick. Have you turned the ice-cream parlour around already?'

Jules lowered his eyes. 'It's not straightforward. Some people are set in their ways.'

Trixie raised her eyes to the ceiling. 'Mavis Lorne will never be told what to do – it's her way or the highway. You did well to give it a go. Let's hope Lady Featherlow sees sense soon. Mavis isn't an asset to Featherlow Bottom; she's a thorn in its side.'

Jules felt like an outsider in a very "inside" place. Trixie might be his salvation. 'Do you trust me, Trixie?'

'Well, let's say, I don't think you're the person you pretend to be. I don't know why – you must have your reasons. I think deep down, you're a good guy.'

Jules held his head in his hands. 'I am here on a mission, but I'm hanging on by the skin of my teeth. Lady Featherlow has a question mark over me, and I desperately need to keep this job. It will lead me to answers.' Trixie noticed Jules's eyes glisten. She nodded – what else could she do? The man was in pain, and she wanted to help him.

*

Jules regained his composure before drifting between tables with an air of confidence that gave no account of his inner anxiety. 'Ted and Bella, what a pleasure to see you both again. That must be three times this week.'

Bella brushed her fingers through her hair. 'Always a pleasure to see you too, Jules.'

Ted grabbed Jules's arm before whispering, 'Are you up for a game of poker in the evenings? We play for good money.'

Jules removed his arm from Ted's grasp. 'Is it an illegal gambling ring?' Ted winked.

Jules sighed. Things were going from bad to worse. Was there nothing that escaped Lady Featherlow's Tea Room?

Bella fluffed up her hair. 'I'm looking forward to tomorrow afternoon's tea dance. I take it you'll be on duty to swing a few ladies around the dance floor?'

Jules managed a weak smile. 'Of course, we've had a significant amount of interest in the event.'

The door to the tea room flew open and Francesca, Archie's wife from the alehouse, ran inside. 'There's an ambulance outside Lorne's Lemonade and Icicles. I hope nothing sinister has happened.' Her gaze settled on Jules. 'I saw you go in there earlier; you didn't stop for long.'

Jules's mouth fell open, and Trixie grabbed the back of a chair. 'It might be Loretta who's been taken unwell. Oh, my goodness, I need to sit down.'

Francesca lowered her eyes. 'Loretta's fine. I was

talking to her when the ambulance turned up. She's as shocked as we are that something's wrong.'

Bella stood up. 'Well, who's looking after the poor woman now? I'll go over to see if there's anything I can do.'

Ted watched as Bella made a quick exit, then rubbed his chin. 'It may not be to do with Mavis. It might be a customer who's fallen ill.'

Trixie gulped. 'I hate things like this.'

Silence fell over the tea room until Bella returned with an update. 'Mavis is dead.'

All eyes turned to Jules, and Francesca blew her nose. 'My dear Lord! God bless her soul. Jules may have been the last person to see her alive. Did she look unwell to you?'

Jules's meeting with Mavis was ingrained on his brain. He was shocked to learn she intended to sue Lady Featherlow. He was also surprised she didn't know Loretta was secretly working at Archie's Alehouse. He rubbed his forehead. 'No. She was perfectly well when I saw her.'

Bella kept her voice low. 'It was an accident. She fell off those ladders she climbed up to reach the top shelf and hit her head on the counter on the way down. A tourist saw her legs poking out from behind the ice-cream cart and phoned for an ambulance. Not a bad way to go if you ask me. She wouldn't have felt a thing.'

Trixie sobbed. 'But what about Loretta? She'll be devastated. She's lived with her aunt since she was a baby.'

Jules stared at Francesca, who was obviously aware that the relationship between aunt and niece was not as it seemed. Francesca blushed as she felt Jules see right through her. 'I must get back to the alehouse. I'll check on Loretta on the way. She's most welcome to stay with Archie and me for a while. We'll help her get through this.'

Jules felt a tremendous sense of relief, not just because Lady Featherlow was no longer at risk of being sued, or the fact that he couldn't possibly work with Mavis Lorne on the shop improvements, he was most relieved for Loretta. Maybe now she would find her voice.

5

THE TEA DANCE

The morning after Mavis's untimely demise, Annabelle visited Loretta. She took flowers and gained some relief in the joy they brought to the young woman. Loretta's eyes lit up at the bunch of pink roses. 'I am so sorry for your loss, Loretta. You must let me know if there's anything I can do to help.'

'That's very kind of you, Lady Featherlow.'

'I'm just on my way over to advise Jules to cancel this afternoon's tea dance as a mark of respect to your aunt.'

Loretta blushed. 'Please don't do that. Everyone's been looking forward to it for weeks. The tickets are sold out.'

Annabelle scanned Loretta's face for signs of pain and upset but, instead, noticed a glow about her she hadn't seen before. 'Well, the decision is yours. If *you* don't mind, then I suppose there's no harm in it going ahead.'

Loretta's smile lit up the room. 'I have absolutely no doubt that the tea dance should still go ahead'. Annabelle thought that was odd, but who was she to temper this young woman's sudden blossoming? Then, when Annabelle was about to leave, Loretta dropped a bombshell. 'Mavis wasn't really my aunt. She told me years ago she was paid highly to take me on as a baby. When I grew up, I became free labour for her. Francesca has helped me gain my confidence; I was planning to build a new life before Mavis died. Now I'm free to do what I want.'

Annabelle gasped. 'Oh, my goodness, you poor woman. How did I not guess that something was dreadfully wrong?'

Loretta beamed the brightest of smiles. 'It's not your fault, Lady Featherlow. Mavis is gone now – everything happens for a reason.'

*

Annabelle paced around her bedroom at Featherlow Manor; she was disturbed. Something wasn't adding up. She reached for the envelope in her bedside drawer and removed Clara's letter. It had made no sense six months ago, and she hadn't even shown it to her husband. Now it left her troubled, she read it again:

Dear Lady Featherlow,

I have a secret I don't want to take to my grave – it's to do with Eleanor Dorrit. I have written to her only to be advised of her passing ahead of me.

Things happened in Featherlow Bottom over thirty years ago that need putting right, and you're the only person who can help.

I am leaving you the tea room in my Will. You need to change the name from mine to yours and make it the best tea room in the country. "Lady Featherlow's Tea Room" has a nice ring to it, much better than "Clara's Cakes".

Once the new tea room is open, things will fall into place. I have a plan to make that happen.

Thank you for helping me rest in peace.

Your loyal servant,

Clara

What things needed "putting right"? Annabelle's head was spinning from thoughts of earlier. Who could afford to pay highly for Mavis to take on a baby?

Giles, the butler, rang the bell for lunch. Annabelle sighed; she wished Winston were here to talk to. Instead, he'd gone off on his yacht for the next six weeks with Freddie and his new wife, Amelie, joining him part-way through his trip. Annabelle had been far too busy with the tea room to join them. She sighed again, then stood up and held her shoulders back. If the secret had been dormant for over thirty years, it surely could stay hidden for a while longer. There was too much to do in the present than to get embroiled in things of the past.

*

By four o'clock, the tea dance was in full swing. The dramatic change in Loretta hadn't gone unnoticed by the residents of Featherlow Bottom. She looked so different in her pale pink dress with shoestring straps and full skirt. A narrow belt accentuated her tiny waist and her long, light brown hair, fell in curls. Loretta's green eyes were sparkling brighter than the glitter ball Jules had erected for the occasion. Archie had been the first to ask her to dance, followed by Sam and then Jonny, a barman at the alehouse. Jules kept track of her out of the corner of his eye. Surely this wasn't the woman he'd spent a silent "picnic" with less than two weeks ago?

Jules had been whisked off his feet too – by Bella and Francesca. However, the conversation with both women begged to differ. Bella's came first during a quickstep: 'Just look at Loretta! That proves to me Mavis was an ogre. I know I shouldn't speak ill of the dead, but it was obvious she suppressed her niece. Loretta's better off without her.'

Francesca was less keen to throw rocks at Mavis: 'I'm so pleased Loretta's putting on a brave face following the sad passing of her aunt. She'll be crying inside. Those two were so close.' Jules frowned. He didn't get the impression Loretta and her aunt were close; from what he'd seen, they were like chalk and cheese. Francesca continued, 'It must have been such a shock to find her aunt at the bottom of those ladders with a broken neck.'

Jules gulped. 'You mentioned yesterday that you were with Loretta when the ambulance turned up. Bella said a tourist had found Mavis.'

Francesca waved an arm in the air in the middle of the waltz. 'It's all so very confusing; I'm in shock. Now let's change the subject to something much more interesting, tell me what brought you to Featherlow Bottom.'

Jules mumbled some words about seeing an advertisement and applying for the job of his dreams, which was untrue. He'd been keeping an eye on the job vacancies in Featherlow Bottom ever since he'd received a letter from someone called "Miss Smith". She'd advised Jules that Lady Featherlow's Tea Room would soon be opening in the village. Miss Smith suggested he got a job there to uncover facts about his past. Jules had got the job but had no idea who Miss Smith was.

Sam asked Lady Featherlow to dance; he enjoyed a foxtrot. 'Are you sure you're not fed up with me staying at the manor house?'

Annabelle laughed. 'You're good company for me, Sam. My husband will be on that yacht of his for weeks. And there's little chance of Freddie and Amelie coming to stay at the manor for the foreseeable future; they're too busy running the business in London – when they're not gallivanting with Winston, of course.'

'Any estimate on when my boat-house will be ready?'

'Well, the builders are aiming for August, so fingers crossed it won't be long. Apparently, it's a simple project in their terms. Mind you; we've put a whole team on the case, so you won't have to wait too long to get back home.'

Sam winked. 'See – I knew you were keen to get rid of me.'

Annabelle blushed. 'Not at all.'

Sam grinned. 'I always knew you ran a tight ship. Once you've completed my refurbishment, then you'll be onto the next one. Lorne's Lemonade and Icicles could do with a makeover.'

Annabelle frowned. Discussions regarding the shop renovations would need to wait until after Mavis's funeral. Then there was Clara's letter; what on earth was going on with that?

Sam held Annabelle at arm's length. 'Something's troubling you. You're more agitated than a bucket of fish. Tell me what's wrong?'

'Have you heard of an Eleanor Dorrit?'

Sam stopped dancing; his face turned grey, and he gripped his chest. 'That's a name from the past.'

Annabelle helped Sam to a chair. 'You're not having a heart attack, are you?'

'Of course not! My old ticker's got a long way to go yet.'

'Well, you obviously knew her. Who was she?'

The colour was coming back to Sam's cheeks, along with a twinkle in his eyes. 'Let's just say we were ships that passed in the night.'

6

THE WAKE

Three weeks later, Archie's Alehouse prepared for a wake. Loretta had arrived early in a plain black dress, and she set to polishing the bar. Jonny caught hold of her hand. 'There's no need to help out today; we've got this covered.'

Loretta shook her head; she'd tied her long hair back on this occasion with a black velvet bow. 'I need to keep busy, what if people find out?'

Jonny leant over the bar and kissed her. 'What if they do? We've got nothing to hide. It was only Mavis Lorne we had to avoid, and please remind me why we needed to do that again?'

Loretta sighed. 'Because I didn't dare tell her I was moving away.'

'And taking me with you.'

Loretta blushed. 'You wouldn't have come to London with me to follow my dreams.'

'I couldn't understand why she had such a hold over you.'

'I've already told you. My mother was a nun, and Mavis did her a favour. What does that make me? A freak.' Loretta lowered her eyes. 'I shouldn't have confided in you. God help me if the story gets out.'

Jonny suppressed a chuckle. That story was too far-fetched for anyone to believe – Loretta was so gullible. As soon as she received an inheritance from her so-called "aunt" he would take advantage of her generosity and make his own way to London. He was a free spirit, always had been and always would be. Luck had been on his side so far with his fleeting romantic encounters, and meeting Loretta was just the icing on the cake.

*

Following a small service at the church, the mourners poured into the alehouse. Loretta had ensured there was enough money for a finger buffet and free bar.

After a few drinks, the locals got talking. Ted and Bella were sitting up at the bar chatting to Jonny. Bella studied the young man, who must be in his early twenties. She admired his chiselled cheekbones, steel-blue eyes, and short sandy hair before airing her opinion, 'You're so good looking, Jonny. You shouldn't be wasting your time behind a bar like this; have you thought about going into modelling?'

Jonny poured Bella another sherry. 'That's certainly my intention. This job's just a stop-gap. I'm on my way to London.'

Francesca strained her ears as she walked past the trio with a plate of sausage rolls. She hovered nearby to listen to Jonny's next revelation. 'Mind you; it's not too bad here at the moment. I have the attention of an older woman.'

Ted leant forward. 'Who might that be?'

'Loretta.' Bella nearly fell off her barstool, and Ted grabbed her leg to steady her. Jonny continued, 'Between you and me, the woman's as mad as a hatter. She thinks her mother's a naughty nun. Her supposed "aunt" had a weird kind of hold over her. I'm sure Loretta's been brainwashed. Still, she'll be in for an inheritance now, so it's not all bad.'

Bella's eyes were on stalks. 'So, Mavis wasn't Loretta's aunt, and the poor girl has a very shameful background – no wonder she keeps herself to herself. I'd do that too if I were in her shoes. Shocking!' Bella tutted and downed her sherry.

Jonny poured her another one and didn't notice as Francesca stormed past them into the kitchen. Archie was in the beer cellar sorting out the pumps. Francesca waited at the top of the steps for him. 'Archie! Come outside with me.'

Francesca looked over her shoulder then stared into Archie's eyes. 'We have a problem. I think I know who killed Mavis. You need to check the CCTV at the appropriate time, and then, if I'm right, we should call the police. I thought Jules might have been involved, and – God forgive me – Loretta herself, but now my bets are on Jonny.'

Archie was used to his wife being over-dramatic. 'We're busy this afternoon with the wake, and tonight the restaurant is full to capacity. I'll check the CCTV in the morning. Don't you worry about it; just leave it with me. We need to make sure we give Mavis a good send-off for Loretta's sake.'

Francesca huffed. 'If you say so. I'll ensure Loretta stays away from Jonny – he doesn't have her best interests at heart.'

Archie winked. 'I'll help Jonny behind the bar, and you make sure Loretta's OK. We've got this covered between the two of us.'

Francesca reached up and kissed her husband of two years. He was twenty-one years older than her and would be seventy next month, but he was young in spirit. She'd been attracted to him for years, from when she'd first worked in the kitchen at the manor house. Archie was the most eligible bachelor she'd ever come across. He was far too handsome with his tall upright stature and silver hair to be single throughout all of his days. Francesca had found him at just the right time, and Archie couldn't believe his luck in attracting the tall, dark-haired beauty.

Francesca went in search of Jules who hadn't turned up at the alehouse. She found him in the empty tea room. 'Why aren't you at the wake?'

Jules shrugged. 'I hardly knew Mavis. I didn't feel it was appropriate.'

Francesca raised her arms in the air. 'Everyone who's anyone goes to a wake or a wedding in Featherlow Bottom. That's why you have no customers this afternoon. You don't need an invitation – you just go!'

Jules jumped at Francesca's authority. 'Just leave your staff to keep an eye on things and come with me – I need you to help me in the alehouse.'

Francesca's manner was one of urgency, and Jules strode after her. 'What do you want me to do?'

'You need to keep Loretta company. I don't trust Jonny; he's spreading rumours about her. I'm worried she's fallen for a rogue. Trust me, the sooner she sees the shady side of him, the better.'

The couple slowed their pace at the sight of a woman approaching the alehouse ahead of them. She was dressed in white with a hat adorned with ostrich feathers. Francesca glanced at Jules, who raised his eyebrows. The lady pushed open the door to the alehouse and, when she walked in, the crowd fell silent. Francesca grabbed Jules's arm, and the couple crept in behind her.

Lady Featherlow attempted to thaw the iciness in the room. 'Hello. Can we help you?'

The lady waved an arm in the air. 'My name is Eleanor Dorrit, and I am here to speak to my daughter, Loretta.'

7

THE AFTERSHOCK

Francesca grabbed Loretta's arm, and Jules stood protectively at her other side. Loretta's eyes popped. 'She doesn't look like a nun.'

Eleanor laughed. 'A nun! Oh no, I'm not a nun. Never have been, never will be. I'm an actor. I tread the boards. My latest show in the West End has just finished. When I heard that Mavis Lorne had finally left this earth, I decided to come for what is rightfully mine – and that's my long-lost daughter.'

There were gasps around the room and several ashen faces among the longer-standing residents of Featherlow Bottom. Sam's mouth had dropped open; Archie leant forward on the bar to try to draw attention away from his great height, and Ted grabbed his wife's hand in an act of unity.

Eleanor scanned the room. 'I recognise a few old faces. It's good to see you all.'

With the scene in the room pressed on "pause", Sam stood up. He walked over to Eleanor and took her arm. 'We need to go somewhere private to talk. I'd invite you back to the boat-house, but it's currently being refurbished.'

Loretta had let go of Francesca and was clinging onto Jules; her fingernails were digging into his arm. He placed a hand over hers in reassurance, before coming up with a suggestion: 'Why don't we go to the tea room? Miss Dorrit and Loretta can speak in there.'

Eleanor nodded, her feathers brushing against the top of Sam's head. As soon as the foursome left the pub the pause button was released: 'What a turn up for the books … I always knew she was up to no good … She's aged well hasn't she? … Why's Sam so keen to help her? … Who is she anyway? … What's all this about a nun?'

Sam and Eleanor walked ahead of Jules and Loretta. Sam poked his head beneath the feathers and kept his voice low. 'I know she's not mine. The dates don't add up. Is she Archie's?'

Loretta shook her head vigorously, and Sam's bald spot took a soft brushing. He leant away from his companion and ran his spare hand over his sparse white hair to ensure no strands were out of place. Somehow in Eleanor's company, he still wanted to look his best.

Once inside the tea room, Jules directed proceedings. 'If you would like to take a seat in one of the upstairs alcoves, I'll ensure you're not interrupted. I'll bring you up a pot of tea. If you require assistance after that, then press the call bell on the edge of the table.'

Eleanor and Loretta headed upstairs, and Jules caught hold of Sam's arm. 'I suggest we leave them to it. It's none of our business.'

Sam rubbed his chin, then nodded. He waited for Jules to take the tea tray upstairs then motioned to the young man to sit down with him on the third step from the bottom of the stairs. Sam whispered in Jules's ear, 'We need to keep nearby in case there's any upset.' Jules nodded and sat down next to his co-conspirator. As luck would have it, with the tea room free of customers and the staff contained in the kitchen, the duo could just about make out the conversation going on above.

Eleanor was the first to speak. 'Oh, Loretta, I'm so sorry for what I did. I put my career first. When I realised I was pregnant, Mavis spotted an opportunity for a potential money earner. She knew I was a wealthy woman. My parents, your grandparents, had died young and left me with a tidy sum. I paid Mavis upfront when you were born and sent her money until you were eighteen.'

Loretta wrung her hands together. 'I'm shocked. At first, I thought Mavis was my aunt. That's what she told everyone in Featherlow Bottom. Mavis said my parents had died in a car crash. It wasn't until I was about fourteen and started asking questions that she lied again and said my mother was a nun and she'd done her an immense favour by taking me on. I've felt like a freak since then. I didn't ask questions after that; I hardly dared speak.'

Eleanor leant forward and grabbed her daughter's hand; her eyes were bulging with tears. 'Can you ever forgive me?'

Loretta felt some comfort from the tearful, soft-featured, perfumed woman sitting next to her. She was nothing like the fearsome Mavis. 'How can I forgive you when I don't know you?'

Eleanor grabbed Loretta's other hand. 'Well let's put a stop to that, shall we? Let's finally get to know each other. Would you like that?'

Loretta nodded, and Jules whispered to Sam, 'It's gone quiet. Are they OK?'

Sam winked before whispering back, 'Loretta will be nodding. It doesn't take noise to do that. You mark my words; those two will be as thick as thieves before long. I should have realised Loretta belonged to Eleanor; can't you see the similarity?'

Jules frowned. 'They're both very pretty.'

'Exactly. Like mother, like daughter. Ssshhh . . . they're speaking again.'

'Now tell me about your hopes and dreams. Have you ever wanted to be an actor?'

Loretta shook her head. 'No! I couldn't think of anything worse.'

Eleanor laughed. 'You've got my way of straight-talking. Surely there's something else you'd like to do other than sell ice-cream?'

Loretta smiled. 'I'm going to London to study floristry. I want to be a florist.'

Eleanor clapped her hands. 'We can go to London together! I'll show you around.'

Sam's mouth fell open, and Jules twisted on the step to face him before whispering, 'I can't see Loretta being at home in London. I'll admit that, since Mavis died, her confidence has grown, but she's much more suited to Featherlow Bottom than the big city.'

Sam squeezed Jules's knee, and he kept his voice low, 'My thoughts entirely, I can't lose Loretta to London, she's been like a daughter to me – not that she's my real daughter of course.'

Jules gathered his thoughts before turning back to face Sam. 'I'll speak to Lady Featherlow. She could suggest to Loretta that Lorne's Lemonade and Icicles is turned into a flower shop. Loretta can study floristry online and go to some practical classes near to here.'

Sam threw an arm around Jules's shoulders and squeezed tightly. 'That's a brilliant idea! Eleanor loves flowers too; she may even stay around to help out.'

Jules blushed. He was taken aback by Sam's show of affection. 'I have to admit I have an ulterior motive; when the ice-cream shop closes, I'll be able to offer knickerbocker glories in the tea room again. It's a win-win situation.'

Sam stood up. 'Come with me back to the alehouse. We'll put your proposal to Lady Featherlow, and then I'll buy you a pint. I don't think those two upstairs are at risk of harming each other; I doubt they'll even notice we've gone.'

8

NEW BEGINNINGS

By the middle of August, changes were taking place in Featherlow Bottom. Lorne's Lemonade and Icicles had transformed into Floral Designs by Loretta. Lady Featherlow had been very supportive of the new business in the village. She had given Loretta the contract to supply weekly flower arrangements to Featherlow Manor whilst she mastered her trade. Eleanor had a natural talent for flower arranging, which surprised *her* more than anyone, and had agreed to settle in Featherlow Bottom until her daughter's new business was running smoothly.

Lady Featherlow's Tea Room was again serving knickerbocker glories, and Trixie was happy to cover for Jules on the odd occasion so he could oversee the building work on the boat-house. Annabelle was racking her brains to find a more suitable job for the charismatic Jules Peridot. He should be using his excellent design skills daily. Still, for now, she needed him in the tea room – business was booming.

Jonny was long gone to follow his dream of becoming a model in London. After a few sharp words from Loretta's mother, he knew he would be wasting his time hanging around for any handouts in Featherlow Bottom. Archie finally got around to checking the CCTV. There was no sign of Jonny entering the ice-cream parlour on the day Mavis fell off the ladders. Archie did see someone else though, and he chose to put that to the back of his mind. There was no point in unearthing the past. Mavis died in an accident. Good riddance was all he could think of. Things were so much better now for Loretta.

Jules reluctantly agreed to go round to Ted and Bella's for a game of poker. He was relieved to find they played for Monopoly money – it wasn't an illegal gambling ring after all. Jules was beginning to warm to the quirky residents of Featherlow Bottom, none more so than Sam – the new boat-house was due to be "launched" tomorrow.

*

Lord Featherlow stood in the woods talking to his wife, 'This is quite remarkable. Did you say that young fellow in the tea room designed it? Well done, Annabelle!

You've certainly had your work cut out while I was at sea on the yacht. Who's the woman with Loretta filling that boat with flowers?'

Annabelle glanced sideways at her husband. 'Eleanor Dorrit. She's Loretta's mother.'

Winston bent forward to take a better look, one hand shielding his eyes from a ray of sun glinting through the trees. 'Well, I never. I'm surprised *she's* turned up again.'

'Do you know her?'

'Let's just say I know "of" her. She set a few hearts alight in her time.' Winston bent forward again. 'Still exquisitely attractive now, I see.'

Annabelle slapped her husband on his arm. 'Why don't *I* remember her?'

'Oh, she was drifting in and out of Featherlow Bottom around the time Freddie was born. You were too busy being a new mother.'

'What do you mean "drifting in and out"?'

Winston smiled at his wife and drew her towards him. 'You must remember the Woodside Theatre. I took you there when we first met – we sat in the Royal Box. Eleanor Dorrit was a touring actor; she performed at the Woodside on many occasions.'

Annabelle laughed. 'It was a run-down building that should have been demolished before we'd even met. Still, I *do* remember the standing ovation we received from the residents when you announced our engagement. Those were the days!'

Lord Featherlow squeezed his wife, and she rested her head on his shoulder. 'I'm pleased you're home, Winston. I have something that's troubling me.'

'What's that, my darling?'

'Clara wrote me a letter. I couldn't make head nor tail of it, and I put it in my bedside drawer. But now that Eleanor Dorrit has turned up, I feel disturbed.'

'What did the letter say?'

'That over thirty years ago there were misdoings in Featherlow Bottom. Eleanor Dorrit and Clara knew about them, and that Clara had received notification Eleanor was dead. The main clue I have is that Clara said everything would lead to the tea room.'

'But Eleanor's not dead.'

'I can see that Winston.'

'Well, what are we going to do?'

Annabelle looked in her husband's eyes. 'We'll do what we always do. We'll keep calm and carry on and, in the process, enrich the lives of the residents of

Featherlow Bottom.'

'What do you mean by that?'

'I have found the perfect architect to design a new theatre for the village. If we have a theatre, then Eleanor Dorrit will never leave. Sam will be delighted, and we may get to the bottom of the misdoings from years ago.'

'Why will Sam be delighted?'

'He's smitten with her, and her with him.'

'Is he Loretta's father?'

'Apparently not. The timing's all out. I wondered at one stage if it was you.'

'ME!!!'

'It was just a thought that crossed my mind briefly.'

Winston bent over in a fit of coughing. Annabelle slapped his back. She could always rely on her husband for something – clarity. Their little chat had been extremely worthwhile; she now had the perfect project for Jules Peridot.

9

THE NEW BOAT-HOUSE

Sam grabbed Jules by the hand and held it in the air. 'This young man has achieved the impossible. He's designed the home of my dreams. If I didn't know he wasn't a sailor, then I never would have guessed. I have a boat outside my front port-hole windows and even a wet room inside. There was many a wet room at sea when a drunken sailor forgot to shut a port-hole. Those were the days!'

There was laughter and cheers all round as the residents of Featherlow Bottom gathered to see Sam accept the keys to his new home. Eleanor and Loretta sat on the side of the boat, which was amass with flowers.

Lord Featherlow stepped forward. 'Here are the

keys to your new home, Sam. We wish you every happiness in the coming years.'

Annabelle pushed past her husband and hugged the old sailor. 'I am so thrilled for you, Sam.' Annabelle lowered her voice. 'I'll miss you up at the manor house. Promise you'll visit.'

Tears welled in Sam's eyes, and he squeezed Lady Featherlow before whispering, 'I promise.'

Sam turned around and unlocked the door to his new abode. He stepped inside and was soon seen waving out of a port-hole to cheers from the crowd.

Annabelle held onto her husband's arm. 'Come along; we should head back home. You can tell me all about your adventures at sea.'

The residents dispersed, and Sam was left alone to enjoy his new home comforts. He sank into a cosy armchair and lifted his legs onto a matching footstool; before long, he had drifted off to sleep.

At first, Sam's dreams were of recent events: The return of Eleanor … the passing of Mavis … the enigmatic Jules Peridot. Sam snuggled into the chair and almost woke himself up with a snore before he fell back into a deep slumber … Jules … Jules … jewels … jewels … the tea room … the peridot falcon … the tea room.

Sam awoke with a start. His heart was pounding. There was nothing else for it – he needed to get to the tea room.

*

Jules was surprised to see Sam so soon after he'd moved into the boat-house. 'Don't tell me you've run out of tea already? I know Lady Featherlow ensured you had a good supply of everything.'

Sam slid onto a bench seat. 'Where is it?'

'Where's what?'

'The peridot falcon.'

'I don't know what you mean.'

'It was my pension fund.'

'I still don't know what you mean.'

Sam sighed as he held his head in his hands. 'I saved a pirate's life when I was at sea, and he gave me the falcon. Covered in jewels it was. I kept it safe for a couple of years or more, but then it was stolen.'

Jules smirked. A pirate? Sam must think he was stupid; he tried to keep a straight face before responding, 'When was it stolen from you? Where from?'

Sam rubbed his forehead. 'Must be over thirty years

ago now. I checked on it every Christmas Day and that Christmas it was gone.'

'Gone from where?'

'My oven.'

Jules took in a sharp intake of breath before chuckling. 'Your oven?'

'Yes. Didn't you hear me? I only use the oven at Christmas. Not much point in making a mess for one. I get a small chicken once a year. The falcon gave me a bit of company at the table – before it was stolen.'

Jules covered his mouth and made an excuse to go into the kitchen. His shoulders were shaking, and his eyes were watering, at the thought of Sam's eccentric behaviour. He took a deep breath and tried to stay calm. It was obvious Sam was deadly serious and distraught. He ordered a tray of tea and cakes and went to sit down next to the old sailor who had lost his falcon.

Sam held Jules's gaze. 'Where did you get your name from? Tell me the truth. I'll know if you're lying.'

Jules dropped his head. 'It has to be our secret.'

Sam held his shoulders back. 'Of course.'

Trixie arrived with the refreshments. Jules thanked her, then focused his attention on Sam. He looked around to check no-one was in earshot. 'I received a letter at the beginning of this year from a "Miss Smith". She said I would find answers to my past in Featherlow Bottom. Miss Smith encouraged me to get a job at Lady Featherlow's Tea Room and said I should use the name "Jules Peridot".'

Sam frowned. 'Do you do anything you are asked to do – even from strangers?'

Jules laughed. 'I'm young, free and single, and struggling to get a job in architecture. What do I have to lose? I'm viewing this as an adventure. I feel quite honoured Miss Smith singled me out. You don't know who she is, do you?'

Sam sipped his cup of tea. 'My best guess is Clara Smith. She used to run this tea room before it was refurbished. Before that she was the nanny to young Freddie Featherlow at the manor house. He's about your age now and running the family business in London.'

'Could you introduce me to Clara Smith?'

Sam shook his head. 'Afraid not. She'd dead. That's two deaths in Featherlow Bottom this year. Let's hope I'm not next – they say they happen in threes.'

The couple sat in silence eating their cakes – there was a lot to digest. Sam wiped his mouth on a serviette. 'How about we help each other? Let's both keep our ears to the ground to see if we can find my falcon. It must still be around somewhere – the clue is in your name. Clara knew where it was. Whilst we're doing that we may establish why Clara summoned you to Featherlow Bottom.' Sam tapped his nose. 'This is a secret mission between the two of us. Is it a pact?'

Jules held out his hand to shake Sam's. 'It's a pact.'

10

POKER NIGHT

Jules was becoming a regular at Ted and Bella's weekly poker nights. He now had more than Monopoly money to tempt him there – their daughter, Lucy, was home following a relationship break-up. Twenty-nine-year-old Lucy was stunning with her shoulder-length blonde hair and pale blue eyes. She was above average height and stood shoulder to shoulder with Jules when she was wearing heels. Jules couldn't believe his luck when Lucy had turned up in the middle of a poker game the week before last.

Bella always made a tray of snacks for the poker players, and since Lucy's homecoming, Jules was keen to help out. The kitchen was small, and Bella sensed she was a spare part. Still, she was pleased her daughter had something to take her mind off things; the charming Jules Peridot was the perfect distraction. Bella left the couple to prepare the snacks on their own.

Lucy turned around and bumped into Jules. 'Oops, sorry!'

Jules grinned down at her; she wasn't wearing shoes in her parents' house. 'I'm not complaining, being accosted by an angel isn't a bad thing.'

Lucy slapped his wrist. She reached into a cupboard below the sink. 'Would you like a drop of whisky in your tea tonight, Mr Peridot?'

Jules's green eyes twinkled. 'Now you're talking.'

Ted yelled from the dining room. 'Calling all poker players. Five-minute warning.'

Jules brushed his hand down Lucy's back. 'Oops, this room is much too small. I'd best be off, or your father will be after me.'

All the regulars were there on that Thursday evening: Sam, Archie, Giles, and, of course, Ted and Jules.

Everyone sat down around the table, and Bella rushed into the kitchen to help Lucy. 'Jules Peridot's quite a looker, isn't he? He's such a nice young man. The tea room has been full since he turned up in the village.'

Lucy glanced at her mother. 'Of course, the tea room could be thriving now because it's had a makeover. I was shocked to see the difference – it was still "Clara's Cakes" when I left home last year. I have to agree, though, Jules is quite easy on the eye.'

Bella winked at her daughter and lifted the tray of drinks. 'I'll take these in. You bring the snacks.'

Lucy allowed herself to run over her little flirtation with Jules in her head . . . before remembering the whisky! She followed her mother into the dining room. Lucy had no idea how Bella had moved the mugs around. 'Now, who's for coffee and who's for tea? I don't know why I ask you all each week; the answer's always the same.' Bella handed Jules his mug of tea first, and he locked eyes with Lucy, who pulled a worried face. Jules took a sip of the hot tea and shook his head. Lucy dashed into the kitchen to fetch the snacks.

It wasn't long before Jules worked out the recipient of the whisky. Giles was unusually chatty. As the butler at the manor house, he was always very discreet, but not tonight. Giles had already mentioned that Lord Featherlow fell off the ladders last winter into a pile of snow. He chuckled at the thought of the Lord attempting to clean the windows. Giles finished his mug of tea and held it aloft for another; Lucy grabbed it and couldn't resist adding a drop more of the good stuff. She handed the replenished mug to Giles and winked at Jules.

Giles's rambling accounts of events at the manor were far more interesting than a game of poker. His eyes darted around the table, and he twisted his hands together as he divulged an occurrence from years ago: 'The return of Miss Dorrit certainly brings back some memories for me. Did you know she came to dinner at the manor with the previous Lord Featherlow?' The poker players shook their heads, and Giles continued, 'His wife and family were all in London at the time. There were only a few of us on duty. Clara was there looking after Freddie, and Mrs Baxter was in the kitchen when she arrived.'

Sam raised his eyebrows. 'Did Eleanor get invited, or did she just turn up?'

'She just turned up. It was one December, and there was a blizzard. Miss Dorrit came knocking at the door complaining she'd been stranded; her chauffeur hadn't arrived. Soaked right through she was. Anyway, Lord Hector Featherlow suggested she stay for dinner.'

Sam couldn't help himself. 'Was she gone by the morning?'

Giles rubbed his head; he was beginning to feel uncomfortable. 'It was such a long time ago; I think she was still there. The Featherlow family remained in London for the rest of the week until the trains started up again. Shocking weather that winter.'

Sam glared at Giles. 'I remember that winter well.'

Bella and Lucy were listening from the hallway. Bella sniffed. 'If I didn't know better, I'd say Giles has been drinking. Either that or he's on some medication that's loosened his lips. Why don't you and Jules offer to walk him home?'

Lucy blushed. 'It won't take two of us.'

'It will take two of you to get him up the steps at the manor house if he's legless by the time he gets there. A bit of fresh air on top of alcohol can send heads spinning.'

Lucy kissed her mother on her cheek. 'You're so thoughtful, Mum. I'll freshen up and grab my shoes. I'll leave it to you to break the news to Giles and Jules.'

Bella walked into the dining room. 'May I have your attention while Lucy's upstairs? It's her thirtieth birthday next week, and we'd like to book a party for her at the tea room. Will Wednesday be OK, Jules? That's the actual day.'

Jules smiled. 'Of course, just let me know the time and for how many.'

Bella nodded. 'Thanks. Oh, and Giles, I need your help too.'

Giles looked startled. 'What with?'

'Mrs Baxter borrowed one of my cookery books, and I need to refer to it tonight. Would you mind popping back to the manor now with Lucy to pick it up? Oh, and Jules, you should go too. It will be getting dark on the way back, and I wouldn't want Lucy walking home on her own.'

Jules stood up and ran a hand through his short black hair. 'Of course, come along Giles, we wouldn't want to upset Bella, would we?'

Bella waved to her departing guests then picked up the telephone to Mrs Baxter. 'Don't ask questions when they turn up. Just give them any old cookery book. Let me know when you're next off duty, and I'll meet you in the tea room for a catch-up, thanks Agnes, you're a true friend.'

11

A PARTY TO REMEMBER

Wednesday had arrived, and the top floor of Lady's Featherlow's Tea Room was reserved for Lucy's 30th birthday party. Mrs Baxter had the day off, and she relished the thought of spending it with Bella. A bit of gossiping was good for the soul.

'Now, tell me, Bella. Why did Lucy's relationship break up?'

'Oh, Agnes, it was no different from the others. My daughter is just so fussy. She'll be coming back home like a boomerang for the rest of her days, unless . . .'

Agnes Baxter stopped blowing up a balloon. She wheezed and took a moment to catch her breath.

'Unless what?'

Bella winked at her friend. 'Unless we get her hooked up with the dashing Jules Peridot.'

Agnes sat down and put her feet up on the bench seat while tackling the rest of the balloons. 'Go on. Tell me what the Tea Room Manager's got going for him that meets with your approval.'

Bella continued to hang banners as she spoke. 'Well, he's the right age, he's single, he's got a good job, and to top it all they've got chemistry.'

Agnes laughed. 'Chemistry! There's no such thing.'

Bella tapped a finger to her nose. 'Trust me. I've got a good feeling about those two.'

*

At three-forty-five, Sam entered Floral Designs by Loretta. He'd offered to escort both mother and daughter to the party and Loretta was keen to shut the shop early for such a special occasion. She'd been rushed off her feet these past few weeks and was excited about seeing Jules again. Loretta had curled her light-brown hair and pinned it up at one side with a diamante clip. She hoped the lemon satin cocktail dress wasn't too much for an afternoon party, but she trusted her mother's advice, Eleanor was always very well turned out.

Bella and Agnes had been at the tea room all day. Jules had provided them with lunch and refreshments, and they couldn't remember a time when they'd had so much fun. The staff at the tea room were lovely. Trixie was always on hand to help whenever they pressed a call bell.

In the kitchen, Trixie downed a pint of water. 'I've lost count of the number of times I've run up those stairs today.'

Jules smiled. 'You're doing a great job. Just view it as a workout. It's not bad when you can exercise and get paid for it at the same time.'

Trixie pinged her boss with a tea towel. 'Well, when my legs give in by five o'clock you can cover for me. Just view it like a trip to the gym.'

The door to the tea room flew open, and Francesca rushed in. She headed straight for Jules. 'I had hoped to pop in earlier. I'm here now, and Archie's on his way. You must let us know if you need any help. We'll be at the party for an hour or so until we need to get back to the alehouse.'

The support of his fellow residents touched Jules. 'That's great, Francesca. Trixie may need a bit of help; we'll repay the favour sometime.'

The door opened again, and Sam walked in with Eleanor holding his arm. Loretta was hidden behind them. When they headed for the stairs, Jules saw her. She looked stunning. He noticed she was still slightly awkward, probably by the fact she was rooted to the spot. He walked over and kissed her on her cheek. 'You look amazing.'

Loretta's sparkling green eyes locked with his. The door opened again, this time for a small crowd to enter. Jules took hold of Loretta's arm and directed her to the foot of the stairs. 'Everyone's up there. I'm on duty for the party, but it would be good to catch up later. I haven't seen you for ages. How's your new business going?'

Loretta smiled. 'It's going well. Thank you for asking. Let's catch up later then.' Loretta turned and made her way up the stairs.

Jules shook his head. Was that really Loretta? The door opened again to the sight of Ted and Lucy. The birthday girl was dressed in a white satin trouser suit. It was a simple outfit which highlighted her pale blue eyes to perfection. Silver metallic sandals with five-inch heels completed the outfit; they were painful to wear but necessary to give her the required uplift to the dizzying height of her latest love interest. Jules held out his hand to shake hers. 'Happy Birthday, Lucy.'

Lucy bent forward and kissed him on the cheek. 'Thank you so much for arranging all of this for me.'

Jules blushed. 'It's nothing. Your mother and Mrs Baxter have been working all day to ensure everything's in place for your big birthday.'

Lucy grabbed Jules's arm. 'Less of the "big". I was in my twenties yesterday; now I'm in my thirties. I still feel seventeen.'

Ted laughed before slapping Jules on the back. 'I had a great time in my thirties. I bet Jules isn't doing too bad either. How old are you now – thirty-nine?'

Jules coughed. 'Thirty-five.'

Ted nodded and looked Jules up and down. 'Good age, that. Good age.' He squeezed his daughter's hand. 'Well, we'd best be off upstairs. It's time for our grand entrance.'

Trixie and Francesca heard the claps and cheers from above. Francesca nudged Trixie. 'Lucy's here. What time are we doing the birthday cake?'

Trixie checked a list on the work surface. 'Five o'clock.'

Something was bothering Sam, and he'd not had a chance to speak to Eleanor since the poker night. 'Do you remember that winter when you were at the Woodside Theatre, and we had dreadful snow?'

Eleanor shifted in her seat before glaring at Sam. 'That was the time we had a blazing row.'

Sam's face dropped. 'I remember. What was it about now?'

Eleanor shook her head. 'Something silly, I imagine. We were young then.'

'You stormed out of the boat-house that evening. Where did you go?'

Eleanor's face clouded over. 'I can't remember.'

At five o'clock, Jules climbed the stairs carrying the cake. Trixie turned the music off, and there were gasps at the candlelight emerging from the dark stairwell. Jules stood in front of Lucy as the crowd sang "Happy Birthday". Lucy blew the candles out and made a wish. Loretta's heart sank when she saw the tall blonde's face aglow as she smiled at Jules. Why was it always so difficult to get what *she* wanted?

By six o'clock, most of the guests had dispersed. Loretta waited downstairs for Sam and Eleanor to appear. She'd had a dreadful time at the party. Lucy had revelled in being the centre of attention and made a beeline for Jules whenever he popped upstairs. He was in the kitchen now; Loretta could see him chatting to Trixie.

The sound of clumping from the stairwell could mean only one thing; Lucy was on her way down. She was three steps from the bottom when she looked up and saw Loretta. 'Loretta! I didn't know you'd come to my party. My feet are killing me. These shoes are just sooooooo . . . '

Loretta jumped up to help the birthday girl who had fallen to the floor. Jules and Trixie ran out of the kitchen and dragged her up to her towering height. With Lucy suffering from nothing more than embarrassment, Loretta sat down on the third step from the bottom of the stairs. She squeezed herself against the wall so that the remaining guests could descend past her.

Jules breathed a sigh of relief when he closed the door after the crowd had dispersed. He headed for the kitchen and noticed Loretta sitting on the stairs. 'What are you doing? Is something wrong?'

Loretta got up and stood next to Jules. 'You have a wonky step. I saw it had become detached, so I sat on it to avoid any further accidents. You'll need to have a look at it before you open up tomorrow.'

12

THE HIDING PLACE

Jules asked Loretta to stay behind, before letting the staff go home early. 'You saved me there, Loretta. Lucy may have sued us for a breach in Health & Safety. Thank you for keeping quiet about the broken step.'

Loretta blushed. 'It's our secret. Do you have a toolbox we could use to repair it?'

Jules strode into the kitchen. 'I certainly have.'

Loretta bent down and gripped the step to check how loose it had become. She was shocked when the whole plank of wood came away in her hand. She held it aloft as Jules arrived with the toolbox. 'It's lucky it was Lucy who dislodged this with her high heels. Heaven help us if Sam or one of the elderly residents had taken a fall.'

Jules rubbed his forehead. 'Well, when you put it like that we've certainly had a lucky escape.' Loretta handed the wooden step to Jules, and he knelt on the floor to assess the best way of fixing it. As he peered over the cavity of the step, something caught his eye. 'Take a look at this. Why would someone put a biscuit tin inside a step?'

Loretta leant over Jules and removed the tin. 'It's very old. Shall we look inside?'

Jules stood up and gestured towards the nearest table and chairs. 'Let's sit down and establish what treasure we've found.' Jules winked at a smiling Loretta. 'I don't care what it is. I want to share it with you.'

Loretta laughed. 'Doesn't it belong to Lady Featherlow, it's her shop?'

Jules grinned. 'I think it's a classic case of finders keepers.'

Loretta blushed – Jules Peridot had an exciting way about him. The tin probably contained stale biscuits. The builders may have left them there by mistake, or as a joke. Loretta was surprised the stairs hadn't been checked over with the recent renovation work. As far as she could remember they'd always been there. Clara used to climb up them to gain access to her apartment.

Loretta nodded towards the tin. 'Well, go on then. Put me out of my suspense.'

Inside the tin, there were two pairs of baby booties: one pink and one blue. There was also a letter. The couple read it together:

My Darling Children,

I knitted these for you, but I couldn't give them to you. I feel a tremendous wrench having left you. Mavis, Agnes, and Clara promised to find you good homes.

I asked Clara to look after your booties in case you ever came looking for me. That way, you would realise I loved you both, and I always will.

Your heartbroken mother,

Eleanor xx

Loretta held her head in her hands. 'I have a twin brother.'

Jules jumped up and paced around the room. 'It doesn't add up. Nothing adds up!'

A stunned Loretta shook her head. 'Why didn't my mother tell me? We've been living together for two months.'

Jules had turned a ghostly shade of white. He sat down and held Loretta's hands. 'How old are you?'

'Thirty-three.'

'I'm thirty-five.'

Jules stared into Loretta's eyes which were the same shade of green as his own. 'I don't think you have a twin, Loretta. I believe you have an older brother.'

Loretta frowned. 'What makes you say that?'

Jules jumped up. 'You need to come home with me now. I have something to show you.'

*

Jules unlocked the door to his tiny, terraced house which was situated up a winding lane on the outskirts of the village. 'Take a seat, while I pop upstairs.'

Loretta looked around the small front room. There was an open fireplace, black leather chair, coffee table and a selection of Grand Designs magazines scattered across the floor. Jules truly lived in a minimalistic bachelor pad. He soon surfaced with a letter. 'Read this.'

Loretta unfolded the letter:

Dear Ben

It isn't my place to write to you, but I don't have long left, and I want to rest in peace.

You must know by now you are adopted. Unfortunately, your birth mother is dead, but your father is still alive. I wrote to your mother recently and received the sad news from her friend. She can't have been gone for long.

If you want to uncover facts about your past, you should apply for a job at Lady Featherlow's Tea Room in Featherlow Bottom. It may take some months from now before it opens. But, trust me, Lady Featherlow will ensure it's a splendid place – better than any tea room in London.

Please use the name "Jules Peridot", that will ruffle a few feathers and solve an age-old mystery that I, for the life of me, couldn't work out. I don't like to leave loose ends. So, in a way, you'll be doing me a favour.

You started off in Featherlow Bottom, and it's only right that you end up there.

Yours truly,

Miss Smith

Loretta stared at Jules. 'That's bizarre.'

Jules sat on the floor. 'There's a chance that Eleanor's my mother too; the three of us have the same eyes. The only thing is, she's supposed to be dead.'

Loretta read the letter again. 'Your name's Ben.'

'Ben Toussaint. My adoptive parents were French. My father was an architect, my mother a lawyer.'

Loretta's eyes widened. 'Were?'

'I lost them both by the time I was thirty. They were older parents, hence the adoption. They left it too late to have a family of their own.'

'I'm sorry for your loss.'

'Don't be. I had an amazing childhood.'

'What do we do now?'

Jules jumped up. 'Let's keep it to ourselves. We need time to think. I'd best get back to the tea room to fix that step. I also need to finish clearing up after the party.'

Loretta jumped up too. 'I'll come with you. I'm used to clearing up after parties; I helped out at the alehouse remember.'

Jules bent down and kissed the top of her head. 'Of course, you did, Sis.'

Loretta giggled. 'We don't know for certain yet.'

Jules smiled. '*I* know for certain. I always wanted a sister. We just need to find a way to make our mother come clean.'

Loretta folded the letter and left it on the coffee table. Both she and Jules had overlooked the scrawled note on the back: *'Tea Room – Third step from bottom.'*

13

REVELATIONS

Giles was racked with guilt. He hadn't had a decent night's sleep since reading the letter Lady Featherlow had left on her bedside table months ago. His time was up. His moment of madness over thirty years ago was coming back to bite him. He sat at the kitchen table and sobbed.

Agnes returned from the vegetable patch with a basket full of potatoes. 'What's up with you? Why are you snivelling like a baby?'

'I need to leave.'

'Why?'

'Eleanor Dorrit.'

'What about Eleanor Dorrit?'

'That night when it snowed. I should have had more self-control.'

'What are you rambling on about?'

'I always knew she found me more attractive than Sam.'

'What?'

'I shouldn't have sinned with Eleanor Dorrit.'

Agnes roared with laughter. 'You didn't sin with Eleanor Dorrit.'

Giles sat up straight. 'But her hat was in my room when I woke up the next morning.'

Tears were streaming down Agnes's face. 'I remember exactly what happened. You drank too much, and Clara and I helped you to your room. We left Eleanor's hat in there as a joke.'

Giles felt a weight lifting from his shoulders – he wasn't Loretta's father. 'Where did Eleanor sleep then?'

'In the blue room. Eleanor was a most courteous guest. She gave Clara and me tips, but you lost out because you avoided her in the morning. Her car arrived before ten o'clock and you hadn't left your room. Clara and I did well to cover for you in front of

Lord Hector; we said you'd eaten something funny. Clara was a hoot; she sneaked into your room and grabbed the hat while you had your head under the covers. Those were the days!'

Giles stood up and held his shoulders back. He looked down his nose at the cook. 'You two shouldn't have been accepting tips.'

'Well, let's just say, Eleanor Dorrit treated the manor like a hotel. Lord Hector didn't know about the tips, so no harm was done.'

Giles's heart was pounding as he strode down the corridor to his room. He wanted everything to do with Eleanor Dorrit out of his life. He couldn't believe how jealous he'd been of Sam Comfrey all those years ago. The woman was nothing but trouble – Sam could have her. She'd been the bane of Giles's life for far too long.

Opening his wardrobe, Giles reached under his jumpers on the top shelf and removed the peridot falcon. He'd only taken it out of Sam's oven in a fit of jealousy when he realised that Eleanor Dorrit preferred the old sailor to him. He'd hidden it away for years, and now he didn't know what to do with it – except put it back from where it came.

*

Sam was annoyed with Eleanor; she was hiding something. It was a warm autumn afternoon, and they sat outside the tea room taking in the sun's rays. He couldn't help himself; he just came out with it: 'Was Lord Hector Loretta's father?'

Eleanor choked on her tea. 'Absolutely not! I can't believe you just asked me that!'

'Well, the dates add up to around the time you stayed at the manor house. I know you turned up there after we had our row – *and* you stayed overnight.'

Eleanor lowered her eyes. 'I was so annoyed with you at the time. It wasn't surprising I fell into the arms of a touring dancer. He was the father, but I can't remember his name. I wonder if Loretta has inherited his ballet skills?'

'It's not funny, Eleanor.'

'I know. What do you expect me to say? I'm not exactly proud of my past. I'm sure you had a girl in every port when you were at sea.'

Sam's eyes twinkled. 'I certainly did. But none of them meant anything. You were always the one for me.'

'We're a good team, Sam. Our paths have taken different routes, but in our twilight years, we still find ourselves together.'

'Does that mean you'll be my girlfriend?'

Eleanor wriggled in her seat; Sam was coming on far too strong. 'No. I'll be on my way again soon.'

'Why?'

'Let's just say, the past will catch up with me if I lay down roots.'

'Are you running away from something?'

Tears welled in Eleanor's eyes. 'I have to keep moving, Sam, that's just the way it is. I hope our paths cross again at some point.'

Sam's heart sank. Eleanor was like a beautiful butterfly. He couldn't catch her – he had to let her go.

*

When Loretta woke up the next morning, there was a note on her pillow.

Darling Loretta

I am so pleased to have spent the last few weeks with you. I am sad that it's time for me to leave again. The theatre's calling me.

Your loving mother,

Eleanor x

*

Sam knew she was gone. She'd picked a flower from the boat and left it propped up in the kitchen porthole. With a heavy heart, he sat at the kitchen table to eat his breakfast. Why was life so difficult? Why couldn't he have fallen in love with someone who didn't have to run away all the time? Maybe if he'd been rich, Eleanor would have stayed around. He'd have been able to take her to the theatre in London and wine and dine her like she deserved.

The sun was shining through the porthole straight onto the glass oven door. Glints of green darted around the room, and Sam held his chest to try to soothe his thumping heart. He couldn't believe his eyes – the peridot falcon had returned. It had found its way back into the oven!

Sam gingerly opened the oven door and took out the lost treasure. He tried to analyse what had happened. Eleanor was gone, and the falcon was back. Had Eleanor stolen it in the first place? Sam checked his front door. It was unlocked. He was annoyed with himself. He always forgot to lock his door; that's why he lost the falcon in the first place. He walked back into the kitchen and stared at the porthole with the white rose wedged into it from outside. Surely, if Eleanor had returned the falcon, she would have brought the rose inside too. No, it wasn't Eleanor who'd stolen Sam's treasure, he was sure of that.

14

THREE HEADS ARE BETTER THAN TWO

Loretta staggered into the tea room before bursting into tears. Jules raised his eyebrows. 'What's wrong?'

'We've lost her. She's gone.'

Jules placed the tray he was carrying onto the nearest table before holding onto Loretta's shoulders. She was shaking, and he wanted to calm her down. 'Don't worry; Eleanor won't have gone far. It's a bit annoying we can't find out yet why she pretended to be dead. There's someone we need to speak to, and that's Agnes Baxter. She's the only one of the baby traders still alive.'

'"Baby traders" that sounds so bad.'

'I know. It was bad.'

'There's a good chance she'll keep tight-lipped about everything. Why would she betray our mother's trust now, after all these years?'

'You're right. I'm sure Eleanor paid highly to keep her three accomplices quiet.'

Sam entered the tea room and Loretta turned to face him. 'Mother's gone away again.'

Sam nodded. 'I guessed that.'

Jules looked at Sam. 'Can I get you your usual?'

'No. I'm not stopping. I just need a quick word in your ear.'

The two men stepped outside, and Sam whispered to Jules, 'The peridot falcon's turned up. Can you believe it?! It's a good job my new oven's got a glass door, or I wouldn't have found it until Christmas.'

Jules whispered back, 'That's amazing! I've had a bit of a breakthrough with my past too. We may not be partners in crime for much longer. You've got your treasure back, and I've established who my birth mother is.'

'Your birth mother?!'

'That's right. I was adopted as a baby. I now know why Clara Smith was so keen for me to work in the tea room. We've found a hidden clue.'

'We?'

'Loretta and I.'

Loretta stepped outside. 'What are we going to do about Agnes Baxter?'

Sam raised his eyebrows. 'Don't tell me that Agnes is Jules's mother!'

Jules glared at Loretta, and she shrugged her shoulders. 'I'd trust Sam with my life. We should share our secret; he may be able to help us.'

Sam's eyes darted from Loretta to Jules, then back again. 'Let's go to the boat-house. We'll be out of the way of prying eyes and ears there. Loretta's right, I'm a good one for keeping secrets.'

Sam unlocked the boat-house door; he was determined to get into a new routine now his treasure was back. He'd left the peridot falcon on the kitchen table while he'd popped out to see Jules. Loretta threw a hand to her mouth. 'Where did you get that from? I saw it only last night; it's so pretty.'

Sam's eyes were on stalks. 'Where did you see it?'

'In Giles's bag, when he walked past the flower

shop at midnight. It was so sparkly under the lamp-lights. I'm never normally up at that time but yesterday was a big day for Jules and me, and I couldn't sleep.'

Sam locked eyes with Jules and made a mental note about Giles. Now wasn't the time to dwell on *his* problems; Loretta and Jules needed help.

Jules leant forward on the kitchen table. 'Where do we start? I have confided in both of you that Clara Smith encouraged me to get a job at the tea room to establish things about my past. You both now know that I'm adopted. For Sam's sake, my real name is Ben Toussaint. My adoptive parents were French, an architect and a lawyer who left things too late to have a baby of their own. I had a very happy childhood, but they both passed away before I was thirty.'

Sam's eyes clouded over. 'I'm sorry for your loss, Son.' Sam glanced at Loretta. 'Neither of you has had it easy, but I'm here now to help. What's the breakthrough you've had?'

Loretta continued the story, 'We found a biscuit tin in the tea room that contained two pairs of baby booties; one pink and one blue. There was also a letter from my mother.'

Sam's heart lurched. 'What did the letter say?'

Jules reached out to hold Loretta's hand. 'That Eleanor gave birth to two babies and Mavis, Agnes and

Clara helped her find homes for them. Look at our eyes, Sam. Loretta and I both have the same green eyes as Eleanor. I'm convinced we're siblings. Why else would Clara Smith reach out to me before she died? The thing we are struggling to work out is that Clara tried to contact Eleanor and received a letter from a friend of hers advising that she was dead.'

Sam had turned as white as a sheet. Everything was falling into place. He knew now why Eleanor had left, why she had pretended she was dead to Clara, why he felt an affinity with the young manager of the tea room, and he guessed why Giles had stolen the peridot falcon. He knew the butler had had a crush on Eleanor; he'd taken the treasure out of spite and finally wanted to clear his conscience.

Sam just needed to do a final check; he looked at Jules. 'How old are you, and what month were you born in?'

'I'm thirty-five, and I was born in March.'

Sam stood up and stared out of the kitchen porthole. He'd always been good at maths. He ran the calculation over in his head a couple of times before turning round to look at Jules. 'If Eleanor is your mother, then I'm your father.'

Jules's mouth fell open. 'How can you be sure?'

'Eleanor had a long stint at the Woodside Theatre

the year before you were born. She was my girlfriend back then. You must be my son.'

Loretta squeezed Jules's hand. 'Are you OK?' She then turned her gaze to Sam. 'Are you my father too?'

Sam lowered his eyes. 'I wish I were, but I'm afraid not. We'd had a row around the time you were conceived, and I found out only yesterday your mother can't remember your father's name. She did mention though that he was a touring dancer; very good at ballet, I understand.'

Loretta's eyes were ablaze as she turned to Jules. 'Our mother has a lot to answer for. No wonder she's disappeared again. She didn't have the guts to let Sam know you are his son.'

Sam defended the love of his life. 'I'm sure Eleanor doesn't know Jules is our son. She tried to cut ties with Clara by pretending she was dead when the past came knocking on her door. Eleanor knew that Mavis had taken on Loretta, but my guess is she had no idea of what happened to Jules.'

Sam didn't like to mention it in front of Loretta, but it would have pained Eleanor the most give up her first baby – Jules – because he was a baby born through love, not one where the father was no more than a fleeting mistake.

Loretta stood up to hug Sam. 'I've always viewed

you as the father I never had. I'd much prefer you to a ballet dancer.'

Sam hugged Loretta back as he blinked away a tear. 'I have enough room in my old ticker for a son and a daughter. Let's hope it keeps ticking for a few more years to come.'

Loretta turned to Jules. 'We need to decide what to do about your name. What should we call you?'

Jules rubbed his face. He was in shock. 'If I have my father's approval, then I'd like to keep it as Jules Peridot. Establishing who my real parents are is a turning point in my life.'

Sam was also in shock. He nodded. The three conniving women must have known about the peridot falcon too. Why else would Clara ask Jules to use that name? He couldn't pick a fight with Mavis or Clara – but he *could* have strong words with Agnes Baxter. It wasn't right he'd been kept in the dark about his son – and his falcon – for all these years. Giles also needed to learn a lesson. What he did was downright spiteful. He should pay for stealing someone's pension fund.

15

IT ALWAYS HAPPENS IN THREES

Sam trudged up the lane en route to Featherlow Manor, he heard a vehicle approaching from behind, and stepped into a gap in the hedgerow to allow it to pass. Sam turned around and removed his cap at the sight of a hearse. After the initial shock, he felt quite relieved. He'd known there would be another death this year, he was just glad it wasn't him. All of a sudden Sam had a lot to live for. After he'd given Agnes and Giles a piece of his mind, his priority would be to find Eleanor. When she was back with her two children, she was sure to become his girlfriend again: they'd all be one big happy family.

Sam looked at his cap; he wondered why he'd taken it off. If the hearse was travelling towards the manor, it was on its way to pick up a body. He'd remove his cap again when it came back down the lane as a mark of respect to whoever was inside.

*

Lady Featherlow's hands were shaking as she put the kettle on. 'This is so upsetting, Giles. Poor you being the one to find Mrs Baxter at the bottom of the stairs. Do you know why she was upstairs in the first place?'

Giles sat at the kitchen table with his head in his hands. He couldn't tell Lady Featherlow that Agnes had threatened him last night, or that she'd come upstairs this morning to question him further about the peridot falcon. Agnes knew he'd stolen it and he'd promised to sell it one day and split the resulting funds between the two of them. They'd managed to keep Mavis and Clara out of the picture to enable a more substantial share each.

Sam had made such a fuss about the falcon going missing at the time, that Giles was surprised Mavis and Clara didn't suspect he was the thief. The butler had found it difficult to hide his guilty conscience whilst in the presence of those nosy women. It was just unfortunate that Agnes wanted her share now; at the point where Giles was determined to clear his conscience and take it back. Things were such a mess!

Annabelle handed a cup of tea to Giles. 'I suggest you take the rest of the day off. You're in shock.'

*

Sam climbed the steps to Featherlow Manor with a sense of trepidation; his finger shook as he raised it to press the ornate brass doorbell. He wondered if he should have gone to the servants' entrance instead, but it was too late – he could hear a chime from inside. Sam was surprised when Lady Featherlow opened the door instead of Giles. He frowned before speaking, 'Was it Giles in that hearse?'

Annabelle shook her head. 'We've had such a tragic morning; Mrs Baxter fell down the stairs, and now she's no longer with us.'

Sam took off his cap again. 'I'm sorry for your loss.'

Annabelle shivered, three deaths this year were just too much. The women were all lifelong friends and much-loved residents in Featherlow Bottom. Tears sprang to her eyes. Sam handed Lady Featherlow his handkerchief, and she took it with gratitude.

'Thank you, Sam. Now, what can I do for you?'

Sam stepped backwards. 'Nothing. I was just out for a walk and saw the hearse. I wanted to check that you were OK.'

Annabelle blew her nose. 'We're fine, thank you, Sam. Winston will be home later, and I've given Giles the day off. The poor man's in pieces – he found her.'

Sam replaced his cap. 'Well, I'd best be off then.'

Sam turned around and headed back down the lane; he needed to speak to Archie.

*

Several of the locals were in the alehouse, and Sam signalled to Archie to join him at a small table in a bay window. 'You'll be getting a request for another wake.'

Archie raised his eyebrows. 'Another one?! That'll be three this year. Who's passed away now?'

'Agnes Baxter. She fell down the stairs at the manor house, and Giles found her.' Sam wondered why Archie's cheeks were flaring up. 'Anyway, enough of that. I have something more important to establish. I need you to check your CCTV for what was going on outside at midnight last night.'

Archie rubbed his chin. 'Why's that?'

'Because Giles is a thief. He stole my peridot falcon over thirty years ago and brought it back last night. Why on earth he decided to bring it back now is beyond me. I will never get to the bottom of it unless I can prove it was him.'

Sam followed Archie into his upstairs office. Sure enough, the CCTV had captured images of Giles walking down the embankment towards the woods at midnight, carrying a bag. Archie leant back in his swivel chair. 'What makes you think the falcon was in the bag?'

'Loretta saw it sparkling under the lamp-lights. Giles walked past her shop before he crossed over onto the embankment and headed for the woods.'

Archie scratched his head. 'I've always thought Giles was a bit shifty. The quiet ones are the worst.' Archie glanced sideways at Sam. 'Can you keep a secret?'

'Of course.'

'Francesca asked me to check the CCTV on the day that Mavis died. Giles was the last person to go into her shop before the tourist saw her legs sticking out from behind the ice-cream cart and called for an ambulance.'

Both men locked eyes. Archie spoke first, 'Mavis fell down the ladders.'

Sam spoke next, 'Agnes fell down the stairs.'

Archie stood up and paced around his office. 'We shouldn't make comparisons and come to the wrong conclusions. What reason would Giles have to want both women dead?'

The office door flew open to the sight of Giles. 'Francesca told me you were up here.'

Sam grabbed Archie's arm. Giles's eyes were on fire. If he'd pushed two women to their death then he wouldn't think twice about finishing off the two men that had worked out his evil doings – the alehouse had stairs too.

Giles closed the door. 'It's not what it seems. You have to believe me. Please sit down; I'll explain everything.'

There was a small meeting table at the end of the room, and all three men sat down. Giles crossed his legs and folded his arms. He stared directly at Sam. 'The women died because of Eleanor Dorrit.'

It was now Sam's turn to have fire in his eyes. 'What?! Don't you go trying to shift the blame, Eleanor wasn't even around when they were murdered.'

Giles sighed. 'They weren't murdered. I went to see Mavis on the day she died because she was blackmailing me. She said I was Loretta's father. I have since found out that I can't be Loretta's father – Agnes and Clara played a trick on me when Eleanor Dorrit stayed at the manor house when it snowed. Anyway, I shouted at Mavis when she was on top of the ladders. I told her to leave me alone. I heard a thud after I'd left the shop but thought she'd dropped a pile of boxes. I had no idea she'd fallen to her death.'

Sam and Archie were calming down, Giles's story was making sense. They waited with bated breath to hear about Agnes.

Giles unfolded his arms and leant on the table.

'Agnes and I had a row last night.' Giles blushed and lowered his eyes. 'It was to do with Sam's peridot falcon.' Giles looked at Sam. 'I'm sorry, Sam. I stole it from your oven all those years ago when I realised Eleanor loved you, not me.'

Sam's eyes twinkled. 'And you decided to return it to me last night. Go on.'

Giles nodded. 'I've lived with guilt for years. When I found out I wasn't Loretta's father I decided to put right the only other thing that was bothering me and that was the falcon. Unfortunately, Agnes knew about the falcon and I promised her years ago I would sell it one day and we'd share the proceeds. I never intended selling it; I just wanted to keep her quiet. As luck would have it, after I had made up my mind to return it to you, Agnes decided she wanted her share. I told her it had disappeared, and she came upstairs this morning with a temper on her like I've never seen before. She was waving her arms around and screaming, and before I knew it, she was rolling down the staircase like a ten-tonne beach ball.'

Sam stifled a chuckle, and Archie sniggered before Giles continued. 'I ran down the stairs to help her, but she was dead on impact with the marble flooring. If the hallway had been carpeted, she'd have had a softer landing.'

Sam reached over and patted Giles's arm. 'Well,

you've certainly been through the mill over the years with all that guilt hanging over you, and those evil women blackmailing you to boot. I've reached my verdict – you're not guilty. Those women stuck together and us men should do the same.'

Giles let out a sigh of relief, and Archie crossed his fingers under the table before asking a question, 'Does anyone know who Loretta's father is?'

Sam nodded. 'Some touring ballet dancer. It was just a one-night-stand.'

It was now Archie's turn to let out a sigh of relief. He stood up. 'I'd best let Francesca know about the wake. Who'll be arranging Agnes's funeral?'

Giles shrugged his shoulders. 'Lord and Lady Featherlow, I guess.' He stood up and pushed his chair under the table, with such a heavy burden lifted from him, he felt ten feet tall.

Sam slapped Giles on the back. 'When you get a new cook, don't go getting into any dodgy dealings. It's best to stay squeaky clean in future.'

Giles held out his hand to shake Sam's. 'Don't worry; my wild days are over.'

Sam grinned. Wild days? He guessed Giles had never had a wild day in his life!

16

ANOTHER WAKE

Ted and Bella sat up at the bar in the alehouse and chatted to Jonny's replacement. They decided that Ivan was a very nice young man. If Lucy and Jules didn't get it together, then Ivan may be an option.

Jules sat at a table in a bay window with his father and sister. He looked at Sam. 'Have you any news on Eleanor yet?'

Sam shook his head. 'I'm struggling to find her. There's a chance, of course, she may turn up today at Agnes's wake.' Jules hoped so, until Eleanor resurfaced, and Jules divulged he was her long-lost son, they had to keep his identity secret.

Lucy strolled over and sat down next to Jules.

'Where have you been hiding since my party? Why haven't you been to poker night?' Jules felt very uncomfortable; he couldn't engage in any relationship until his past was out in the open. What would everyone say when they found out Sam was his father and Loretta his sister?

Jules smiled at Lucy. 'I've been snowed under at the tea room. Business is still booming even though we're now well into October. I thought it might drop off after the summer months.'

Lucy dropped her head onto Jules's shoulder, and Sam and Loretta flinched. 'Well, it will be down to your charisma and good looks.' Lucy noticed Loretta narrow her eyes and was even more determined to win the dashing Jules Peridot's affection. He was getting far too close to the boring Loretta for Lucy's liking.

Lady Featherlow wandered over to speak to Loretta. 'Thank you so much for doing the flowers today. They were amazing. You did Mrs Baxter proud.'

Loretta's cheeks flushed a pretty shade of pink, and Lucy saw Jules reach over to squeeze Loretta's hand. Did the man have no sensitivity? Here she was with her head on his shoulder, and he was holding another woman's hand. Lucy's patience was about to run out. She lifted her head, leaving long blonde hairs on Jules's jacket. 'If I'm in the way here, I'll go and join my parents up at the bar.'

Jules watched as Lucy wandered off. Being incognito was ruining his love life. There must be a way to track Eleanor down. With the seat now vacant next to Jules, Lady Featherlow asked if she may sit down.

'I want to have a word with you, Jules. You did such a good job with the design of Sam's boat-house that Lord Featherlow and I were wondering if you'd like to design a theatre.'

Sam raised his eyebrows. 'A theatre?'

Annabelle smiled. 'Yes, Sam. You must remember the Woodside Theatre. Well, it's about time we resurrected it.'

Sam rubbed his hands together. 'I can't think of a better idea!'

Jules gulped. 'I can't design a theatre. The boat-house was a challenge for me. I have a degree in architecture, but no practical experience.'

Sam leant forward. 'This is your opportunity, Son. Grab it with both hands.'

Annabelle grinned. 'Sam's right. I'll ensure you shadow an experienced architect, but I'll request you have a say in the design. It will look good on your CV.'

Jules's heart was pounding. Clara bringing him to Featherlow Bottom wasn't just impacting on his past life it was affecting his future. 'What about the tea room?'

'Oh, I can find another manager for that. Jobs in Featherlow Bottom are never vacant for long. We have a new cook at the manor already; her name is Miss Floris.'

Loretta smiled. 'That's a pretty name.'

Annabelle agreed. 'Yes, it is. She's called Miss Ellie Floris to be precise. She's young like you and Jules. Winston and I have never tasted some of the concoctions Ellie is creating. She worked in a Michelin Star restaurant previously. Fingers crossed, so far so good – Giles has taken a real shine to her. It's like father and daughter whenever I pop into the kitchen. There's always a bit of banter going on. It's lovely to see.'

Sam felt pleased for Giles. He deserved a bit of happiness in his latter years. Annabelle glanced over at Loretta. 'Is there any news of your mother, my dear?'

Loretta shook her head, and Sam's chin sank into his chest. Annabelle frowned; there must be something she could do to help.

*

That evening, after the wake, Annabelle sat at her husband's desk in the study. She composed two vacancy notices: the first one for a Tea Room Manager;

the second for a Head of Amateur Dramatics. It would be a while before the theatre was built, but the job of the Head of Amateur Dramatics would be to give input on the design work and to establish Featherlow Bottom's first Amateur Dramatics Society.

Annabelle would post the vacancies online and wait for Eleanor Dorrit to contact her. There was no way Eleanor would pass up the chance of a dream job. Annabelle had to admit she was doing this for Sam more than herself. He looked so sad this afternoon. It was sweet that he'd called Jules "Son". Annabelle placed her pen down on the desk. Now there was a thought. Surely not? She had to admit Loretta and Jules both had the same eyes – the same brilliant green colour as Eleanor's.

Annabelle smiled to herself. She loved it when a plan came together. Now, why hadn't she worked out before that the dashing Jules Peridot had turned up in Featherlow Bottom in search of his parents? Annabelle picked up her pen again. She was more determined than ever to track down Eleanor Dorrit. There was no time to waste.

17

THE APPLICANTS

One week later, Lady Featherlow was swamped with applicants for both vacant positions. She scanned all the names for Eleanor Dorrit to no avail before leaving all the actor's CV's in a pile. Only one applicant would suit that position – if Eleanor didn't turn up, there would be no role.

There was one application for the Tea Room Manager vacancy that intrigued her. Annabelle phoned the candidate immediately. 'I can't believe you've applied for the vacancy! Your background isn't perfect, but I know you will suit the role. Featherlow Bottom will be lucky to have you. When can you start?'

*

Annabelle walked into the tea room with a spring in her step. She headed straight for Jules. 'Your replacement will be here in two weeks. I'm not going to divulge who it is at the moment, but I'm thrilled with my choice.'

Jules's face dropped, and Annabelle patted his arm. 'You're far too good for this role. Once you've given a handover to your successor, you will be free to follow your dreams. Your parents will be so proud of you.'

Jules frowned. What was Lady Featherlow going on about? He hadn't mentioned any parents to her. His adoptive ones had passed away and the only people who knew about his birth parents – now that Clara, Mavis, and Agnes were gone – were Sam, Loretta, and Jules himself.

Annabelle waved to Bella, who was sitting alone drinking her tea. 'Excuse me, Jules. I should catch up with Bella.' Annabelle sat down next to the glum-looking resident.

'You look sad today, Bella.'

Bella sniffed. 'I miss Agnes; we used to come in here for a bit of a gossip. If there's anything you need to know, then you can always find it out in the tea room.'

Annabelle raised an eyebrow before asking, 'You

don't know where Eleanor Dorrit went do you?'

Bella placed her cup on its saucer and sat up straight; she felt quite important. 'My best guess is France.'

Annabelle spluttered. 'France!! Why on earth would she go there?'

Bella glanced behind her then scanned the room before speaking quietly, 'Agnes didn't give me all the details, I just know there was a pact between her, Mavis and Clara and it involved Eleanor Dorrit.'

Annabelle leant forward. 'Go on, tell me more.'

'When Eleanor Dorrit was last here, Agnes let something slip. Ted and I were sat at the next table, so we managed to have a good listen in. We were sharing one of Jules's knickerbocker glories – they've been a great boost to the menu offering by the way.'

Annabelle was becoming impatient. 'What makes you think Eleanor Dorrit is in France?'

'I overheard Agnes say: "His parents were French". Now I don't know whose parents were French, but Eleanor became quite upset. She turned into a snivelling wreck. She took off again soon after that.'

Annabelle was about to stand up when Bella remembered something else. 'Now, if I remember rightly, Agnes mentioned a name, now what was it?' Annabelle wrung her hands together and waited while Bella channelled her thoughts. 'Ben Toussaint. That was it! Ben Toussaint.'

Jules caught the tail-end of Bella's ramblings as he took orders from a nearby table. He could feel Lady Featherlow's stare burning into his back. She knew. Lady Featherlow had worked out he was fake. He turned to face her head-on. Instead of finding his boss with a livid expression on her face, she was smiling at him with great compassion. She stood up and walked over to him. 'We need to talk. Come to the manor at seven o'clock tonight.'

*

Giles brought a tray of canapés into the drawing room. 'Ellie made these when she knew Jules was visiting. She wanted to impress a fellow caterer. Would you like some tea to go with them?'

Annabelle glanced at a bewildered Jules and shook her head. 'I think a drop of champagne is called for – we're celebrating Jules's new job. Just two glasses will do.'

Jules felt awkward divulging the details of his past to Lady Featherlow without his father and sister knowing, but they all needed help. It wasn't as if he'd broken any confidences – Lady Featherlow had worked most of it out for herself.

Annabelle was entranced to learn about the booties and letter in the biscuit tin. However, she cringed at the thought of Health & Safety issues in the tea room. It was a good job Lucy hadn't worked out the step was faulty – she may have tried to sue. So, Jules was really Ben Toussaint. He said he'd spent all his life in England and that Eleanor Dorrit wouldn't find him in France. He was here now, trying to find her.

Jules held his arms in the air. 'What are we going to do?'

Annabelle called for Giles. 'Two more glasses of champagne please, Giles.'

Giles was surprised the tray of canapés remained untouched. He sensed Lady Featherlow and her visitor were agitated. Giles closed the door slowly, hoping to catch a snippet of conversation that may reveal why there was so much tension in the room. He was in luck; Lady Featherlow let out a sigh before speaking: 'There must be some way we can track Eleanor Dorrit down.'

Giles returned to the kitchen and opened the cupboard containing Mrs Baxter's recipe books. There! He knew he'd seen it somewhere. He replenished the champagne flutes and tucked the book under his arm before returning to the drawing room.

Jules sat with his head in his hands. 'We have to

find her soon, more for Sam's sake than anyone's. I'm worried he'll die of a broken heart.'

Annabelle gasped. 'We can't have another death in Featherlow Bottom this year!'

Giles handed over the champagne flutes. He then opened the front cover of the cookery book before handing it to Lady Featherlow. Inside the hardback cover Mrs Baxter had scribbled a note:

Eleanor Dorrit – 06789-667112

Lady Featherlow stared at Giles. 'How long has that note been there?'

Giles held his shoulders back. 'I was at Ted and Bella's for a social evening when Bella requested me to return to the manor to collect her cookery book from Mrs Baxter. Jules will remember, he was there at the time. Anyway, the book Mrs Baxter gave me was this one. It turned up again about a week later, and I looked inside to see what was so special about it. That's when I spotted the name and number.'

Annabelle's eyes widened. 'So, Bella's in on all this too?'

Giles wasn't sure what "all this" was. 'All I know, Lady Featherlow, is that I gave the book to Bella's daughter and shortly before Mrs Baxter died she met Eleanor Dorrit in the tea room. Mrs Baxter came back with the book. I knew it wasn't Bella's book in the first place; it's been in the kitchen cupboard for years. I sensed people were playing tricks on me – it's happened before.'

Annabelle held the book to her chest. 'I will need to keep this for a while, Giles. You've been very helpful. I'll ring the bell if we need anything else.'

Jules sat on the edge of his seat as Lady Featherlow phoned the number.

'Hello.'

'Eleanor, it's Annabelle Featherlow.'

'Oh, hello, Lady Featherlow.'

'Where are you?'

'In London.'

'Why aren't you in France?'

'Why would I be in France?'

'Why haven't you applied for the job of your dreams in Featherlow Bottom?'

'I've no idea what you're talking about, Lady Featherlow. I've been feeling a bit under the weather these last few weeks, and I've been resting up.'

Annabelle threw her hand to her chest. 'Tell me

your address. I'll send a chauffeur to pick you up. You need to come home straight away.'

'Home?'

'Yes. You need to come home to Featherlow Bottom.'

18

ALL IS REVEALED

The following afternoon, Eleanor walked up the steps into Featherlow Manor. Giles took hold of her overnight bag and showed her into the drawing room. Annabelle stood up and held her arms open wide before stepping forward to hug her guest. 'You poor woman. I can't believe how much heartbreak and trauma you've been through over so many years. Well, I'm here now, and I'm going to put everything right.'

Eleanor frowned as Lady Featherlow linked arms with her and led her to a chair next to the fire before reaching for a pink cashmere throw and tucking it around her legs.

Annabelle sat on a footstool and held Eleanor's hand. 'Firstly, you must tell me why you've been feeling unwell these past few weeks. Winston and I are acquainted with the finest doctors in the country. We will ensure you receive the best care.'

Eleanor didn't know whether to feel comforted or annoyed. She decided on the latter before removing the throw and standing up. 'I don't know what you think you know, Lady Featherlow, but there's nothing wrong with me. I've just been a bit down in the dumps.' Eleanor lowered her eyes before continuing, 'Let's just say there are some things in my past that come back to haunt me now and again. Don't you worry about me, I always bounce back.'

Annabelle stood up too. 'That's excellent! You'll take the job then?'

'What job?'

'Head of Amateur Dramatics. I've built the role around you. We're resurrecting the Woodside Theatre, and it would be perfect if you could work with Jules who will be helping to design it. Featherlow Bottom needs an Amateur Dramatic Society; I want you to establish one then head it up.'

Eleanor laughed. 'Jules, the Tea Room Manager? You're joking, aren't you? He's not capable of designing a theatre. Have you been on the sherry?'

Annabelle was offended. 'He designed Sam's boathouse.'

'That's not much more than a glorified shed. Now, will you tell me what's really going on? Why have you dragged me back here?'

Annabelle snapped, 'Because your son needs you.'

'My son?'

'Yes. The one you left with Clara, Mavis, and Mrs Baxter to re-home thirty-five years ago. The baby son you never told Sam about. I am offering you the chance for a new life here. One where you can spend the rest of your days with your son, daughter and the love of your life.'

Eleanor's knees buckled beneath her, and she grabbed the chair arm before sitting down again. 'My son's looking for me?'

'He certainly is.'

'But what about his adoptive parents? Agnes told me they're French and that he was named Ben Toussaint.'

Annabelle sat back down on the footstool and reached for Eleanor's hand again. 'Unfortunately, your son lost his adoptive parents before he was thirty. They were a lot older than you and Sam. They gave him an excellent upbringing though; he's turned into a charming young man.'

Eleanor blushed. 'Does he look like me?'

Annabelle nodded. 'He has the same sparkling green eyes as you and Loretta. I should have worked out long ago that you three were related.'

'Well, if he's been looking for me, then I suppose that's a good sign.'

Annabelle squeezed Eleanor's hand. 'I know you're worried about what Sam will say, but I can assure you he's over the moon to have met with his son. Loretta's thrilled too to have a brother. The only person missing now in your lovely family is you; they are desperate to find you so that you can commence a new life together.'

Eleanor took a deep breath before standing up. 'Then there's no time to waste. Where can I find them?'

'They're waiting for you in the boat-house.'

'Well, I'd best get over there then. I hope Ben approves of me when he meets me.'

Annabelle grinned. 'He's met you already, and he's delighted you're his mother. Oh, and by the way, he's changed his name to Jules – Jules Peridot.'

Eleanor threw a hand to her heart. 'Oh, my goodness! He's turned into a strapping young man. What brought him to Featherlow Bottom?'

'It was Clara who wanted to clear her conscience before she passed away. She kept the pink and blue booties you knitted for your babies, and the letter you wrote for them. Jules and Loretta found them in a biscuit tin in the tea room, and everything unravelled from there.'

Eleanor smiled at Lady Featherlow. 'It took me ages to knit those booties; I'm not cut out for knitting.'

Annabelle laughed. 'I'll arrange for the chauffeur to drive you to the woods. And, trust me, your son has the potential to be an amazing architect. He's got a degree in that field.'

'A degree? Well, I suppose I'll find out how good he is when we work together on the design of the new theatre.'

Annabelle smiled. 'Does that mean you'll accept the role of Head of Amateur Dramatics?'

Eleanor held out her hand to shake Lady Featherlow's. 'I'd like to accept it very much. Thank you for everything, Lady Featherlow.'

Giles stood by the open front door of the manor as Eleanor descended the steps. She remembered something and reached for her purse. Eleanor turned back and handed Giles a ten-pound note. 'It was only a short stay, but it was delightful. Thank you, Giles.'

19

THE REUNION

So much had happened since yesterday. Jules had advised his father and sister of Lady Featherlow's intervention and, from that point forward, it was all hands on deck to clean the boathouse, stock the cupboards, fill the fridge, and tidy the clearing in the woods that surrounded it. Autumn leaves were on the ground, and Loretta sent Sam outside to sweep them up.

Jules hurried through the door with the last bucket of flowers from Loretta's shop. He caught his breath before speaking, 'Lady Featherlow called. Eleanor's on her way – she'll be here any minute!'

Sure enough, a glint could be seen at the top of the footpath that led to Sam's dwelling. Sam squinted and placed a hand on his chest to soothe his thumping heart. 'That's Lord Featherlow's car up there. I'd recognise it anywhere; it's the shiniest one in the village.'

Loretta grabbed the remaining flowers from the bucket and arranged them in a vase. She moved the peridot falcon off the kitchen table and looked for a better place for Sam's prized possession – it needed a prime spot. Loretta took the sparkling bird into the lounge and placed it on the mantelpiece above the fireplace. At the sight of their mother walking down the path, Jules and Loretta rushed to open the door. Sam lagged behind them and grabbed the falcon. He dashed into the kitchen and hid it in a cupboard.

Loretta hugged Eleanor. 'Mother! You're home! Can you believe that Jules is your son? We're going to be such a happy family now.'

Loretta stepped aside, and Eleanor stared at Jules. She looked him up and down from all angles before smiling her approval. 'I should have guessed you were a Dorrit.'

Sam stepped forward, rubbing his chin. 'He's a Comfrey too.'

Eleanor blushed at the sight of Sam. She never thought this day would come. He appeared to be acting normally, that made it easier for her to do the same.

She felt a tremendous weight lifting from her whole body.

Jules stepped forward and held out his hand to shake Eleanor's. 'It's good to see you again Miss Dorrit.'

Eleanor held out her arms for Jules to walk into them. 'Please call me "Mother".' She held onto Jules for a good while before stepping back with tears in her eyes. 'That's of course if you want to.'

Jules warmed to Eleanor in an instant. He could tell she was doing her best to hold things together on the surface; she must be traumatised inside. His mother had received the astonishing news about him from Lady Featherlow less than an hour ago.

Jules took hold of her hands. 'I would love to call you "Mother". I have never called anyone by that name before. My adoptive parents were French, and they preferred me to call them "Maman" and "Papa".'

Loretta turned to Sam. 'What should we call *you*? I know you're not my real father, but I've always wished you were.'

Sam coughed. 'Just plain old "Sam" will do. I'm too set in my ways now to get used to answering to anything else.' He coughed again and shuffled his feet. 'I'm happy to be your father though – that's to both of you, of course.'

Eleanor's heart flipped. Why did she think Sam would be annoyed with her? She should have told him years ago about her babies. Maybe it wouldn't have taken this long for them to become united. Still, everything happens for a reason – perhaps now was their time to be a family.

Eleanor walked into the kitchen. 'I'll put the kettle on.'

Jules placed an arm around Loretta's shoulders. 'I like her.'

Loretta glanced up at her brother. 'I like her too.'

Sam dashed into the kitchen behind Eleanor and closed the door. She turned around to face him. 'Am I forgiven?

Sam shrugged his shoulders. 'There's nothing to forgive. We're all here now aren't we?'

Eleanor nodded before opening a cupboard in search of teacups. She gasped before turning around. 'It was YOU who stole it! After all these years it's turned up in your cupboard.'

Sam's eyes darted towards the door to the lounge, and he pressed a finger to his lips. 'Ssshhhh! I told our son I saved a pirate's life, and he gave it to me as a reward. That peridot falcon is my pension fund. Not only that, but it was also stolen from me for years. I only got it back three weeks ago. We can travel the world now, Eleanor. I'll sell it and give you the life you deserve.'

Eleanor tutted. 'I'm shocked Jules believed your story about a pirate – how could he be so naïve?'

Eleanor took the falcon out of the cupboard and turned to face Sam, whose head was hanging low as he shuffled his feet. Eleanor sighed. 'We can't sell the falcon, Sam. It is far too valuable for that. It's special to us – we have to keep it in pride of place somewhere. Why travel the world when everything we need is here?'

Eleanor walked back into the lounge. She looked around, then placed the falcon on the mantelpiece above the fireplace. Loretta scratched her head; she was sure she'd put the sparkly ornament on there earlier. Eleanor turned to face her children. 'I need to tell you about my new job. I'll be working with you, Jules, on the design of the new theatre. I'll also be heading up an Amateur Dramatic Society. I'll help out in the flower shop when I can, Loretta, don't you worry about that.'

Sam entered the lounge with a tray of mugs and a plate of custard cream biscuits. 'I've made the tea. You have a sit-down, dear, and put your feet up. You've had a long day.'

Eleanor sank onto the sofa and Jules pushed a footstool under her legs. She bit into a biscuit and reflected on that day over thirty-five years ago when she'd been on stage at the Woodside Theatre. The peridot falcon was one of the props. Sam was in the audience the night it went missing. They'd been for dinner after the show, and Eleanor had joked about finding a rich husband. She regretted doing that as soon as the words slipped out. The look on Sam's forlorn face confirmed to her that she didn't need a rich husband at all. Sam had given her more than money could buy; he'd given her his heart.

Loretta turned on a lamp next to the fireplace. Eleanor glanced across at her children chatting to each other, and her heart leapt at their sparkling green eyes. She never thought she would see this day. The theatre prop was twinkling on the mantlepiece too. Eleanor shivered at the sight of the eerie-looking bird that had caused so much trouble. The falcon was made from plaster and fake gemstones; it wasn't adorned with peridots, emeralds, or anything of value in green – it was covered in expertly crafted glass.

20

THE NEW MANAGER

It was Monday the 1st of November and Lady Featherlow arrived at the tea room early. She unlocked it with her own set of keys, turned the alarm off, and sat down at a table next to the downstairs windows. She couldn't remember a time when she'd been so happy. Clara Smith must have been a white witch. By craftily leaving the tea room to Annabelle in her Will she'd turned around the lives of so many. She'd brought one family back together, and now another family was about to be reunited – Annabelle's family.

When her son, Freddie, had married Amelie after a short engagement, Annabelle had hoped they would be spending more time in Featherlow Bottom. However, business commitments with the family firm had kept them in London, and Winston's yacht wasn't helping either. They'd had weeks away on it this year as part of an extended honeymoon. Still, things were turning around now. Freddie had called last night to say he was planning to move the Global Headquarters of Featherlow Forbes Menswear to Featherlow Bottom. They would keep the London Office, but Freddie was feeling homesick.

Annabelle had a good view of the ornate footbridge and lamp posts lining the embankment from the tea room window. Her thoughts turned to Friday; they should take the wrought iron tables and chairs outside for the revellers to use on Fireworks Night. Archie's Alehouse was planning a barbecue with live music. A few extra seats along the embankment wouldn't go amiss. Annabelle made a mental note to remind Jules to do that. She was deep in thought when she saw someone waving through the window. She jumped up and opened the door.

'Fifi!! I can't believe you're here.'

Annabelle held her arms out wide, and Fifi walked into them to hug her. 'I'm so excited about this, Lady Featherlow. The timing couldn't be more perfect. I can't believe it was nearly a year ago since we were last here for the Featherlow Forbes Christmas Spectacular at the manor.'

Fifi waved her left hand in the air. 'It's official.

Grant and I are finally married. It was a long engagement – ten whole months!'

Annabelle wiped away tears of laughter. 'I have missed you and Amelie so much. Freddie advised me last night he's moving the Headquarters to Featherlow Bottom. Oops, should I have mentioned that?'

Fifi grinned. 'It's fine, Lady Featherlow. Grant and I were expecting that to happen. Obviously, as Freddie's Executive Assistant, Grant will need to move down here too. The timing of this job is perfect for me. I fancied a change from working on reception. The offices here will be smaller than the ones in London; I'd have been bored without too much going on.'

Annabelle squeezed Fifi's arm. 'You are a people person. The tea room is lucky to have you. There will be a two-week handover with Jules, the current manager, but he won't be going very far if you need his help. I've worked a shift in here myself – so I know the ropes. I'm not very good at it though. I didn't realise the stamina that's required.'

Fifi laughed. 'Well, I've got stamina by the bucket-full. Where do you want me to start?'

'Have you got a pad and pen on you?'

Fifi rummaged in her bag. 'I certainly have.'

'Well, the first thing is to ask Jules to place our

wrought iron tables and chairs along the embankment on Friday before we close.'

'Noted. What's happening on Friday night, then?'

'It's the 5th of November, Fireworks Night. Winston's arranged for rockets to be launched from the manor grounds and Archie's providing a barbecue for the residents. I thought a few extra tables and chairs would be of use.'

Fifi's baby blue eyes twinkled. 'That's so nice! I'm sure Grant and I will be really happy living here.'

Annabelle's eyes widened. 'There's so much happening at once. You *do* realise the job doesn't come with accommodation, don't you? We renovated Clara's apartment to provide more seating upstairs. Where did you stay last night? You surely didn't travel down this morning.'

Fifi smiled. 'There's no need to worry, Lady Featherlow. I'm staying in a nice little bed & breakfast in the next village. Grant says he'll be able to move down soon and then we'll look for a house.'

Annabelle was aghast. 'You must stay with us until you find a new home!'

Fifi blushed. 'That's far too kind of you, Lady Featherlow. I'm sure we'll be sorted soon; the B&B will do just fine for now.'

The door to the tea room opened, and Jules walked in. He smiled at the young blonde woman sitting next to Lady Featherlow. Her pixie cut framed her pretty face to perfection. Fifi stood up. 'You must be Jules Peridot. I've seen your photograph on the website. I'm Fifi McGuire, Mrs Fifi McGuire, recently married, not looking for fun. I'm here to replace you. Where are you off to, anyway?'

Jules's jaw dropped, and Annabelle laughed before standing up and pushing her chair under the table. 'I can see you two will get on. I'll leave things in your very capable hands. You know where I am if you need me.'

*

At the Global Headquarters of Featherlow Forbes Menswear in London, Grant opened the door to Freddie's office. 'I've just had a text from Fifi. She's started her job at the tea room today. Any idea when we'll be able to escape to the idyllic surroundings of Featherlow Bottom?'

Freddie leant back in his chair. 'The sooner, the better. I'm fed up with Amelie still working in the Marketing Department. Her new boss is even more charming than the last. It's brilliant news that Fifi spotted the tea room role. It won't be such an upheaval for Amelie to move away from London now. She'll be lost without her best friend.'

Grant flashed a dimpled smile. 'Fifi says your father's setting off rockets on Friday night from the manor grounds and that Archie's providing a barbecue for the residents.'

Freddie combed his fingers through his shiny black hair. 'I've been away from home for far too long. We should get the train down to Featherlow Bottom on Friday to surprise my parents.'

Grant punched the air. 'Great idea! I'll let Fifi know we're coming down and ask her to keep it quiet.'

21

ROMANCE IN THE AIR

By Friday, Fifi had met most of the regular customers. Jules was good at showing her the ropes, but Trixie was best at filling her in on the gossip. With the news that Grant, Freddie and Amelie were coming down for a long weekend, things couldn't get much better.

Fifi felt a tug on her apron. She turned round to see Sam with a twinkle in his eye. 'I need a favour. I'm planning something for tonight, and I don't want the locals to know about it. It's difficult because I'm well-known in the village, and the folk in Archie's Alehouse do nothing but gossip. As you're new, you're the only one I can trust with my secret.'

Fifi felt honoured. 'Just let me know what you need me to do, I'm at your disposal.'

Sam tapped his nose. 'I don't want Lord and Lady Featherlow to know either. I got in a bit of trouble once with a naked flame.'

Fifi suppressed a chuckle as she edged along the bench seat next to Sam and took out a pad and pen from her pocket. 'I'm ready and waiting. Nothing's too much trouble for you, Sam. Just fire away.'

'I need a fleet of boats – just small one's mind – and some candles. I've checked the wind speed for tonight and have decided to give it a go.'

'What are you "giving a go" to Sam?'

'I'm going to propose to Eleanor Dorrit. I should have done it years ago.' Fifi threw her hand to her mouth. She waited for Sam to articulate. 'The way I see it is: The fireworks will go off at eight o'clock, so I want the boats to start floating down the river with the candles from seven-thirty. I'll bring two deckchairs from the boat-house and set them up near the bridge. When I'm sitting there with Eleanor, she will see the boats floating through from under the bridge, and then I'll propose. The fireworks will start up soon after that.'

Fifi's mouth was wide open. She'd not been taking notes – this was soooo romantic! Sam tapped his teaspoon on the side of his cup. 'Are you listening?'

Fifi sprang into action. 'I'm listening. No need to bring deckchairs; Lady Featherlow has requested the wrought iron tables and chairs to be placed along the embankment tonight. I'll reserve you your very own table.'

Sam nodded. Fifi was a quick thinker. 'And what about the boats? Don't go making paper ones and putting candles in those or we'll be heading for disaster.'

Fifi rubbed her forehead. 'I'll sort everything. Just bring Eleanor to the bridge for seven-thirty and sit down at the reserved table. All you need to do is focus on making the proposal extra-special.'

'Isn't a fleet of boats "extra-special"?'

Fifi smiled. 'Of course, it is, but you will need to think of some words too.'

Sam made his way out of the tea room, and Fifi phoned Grant. 'Where are you?'

'We're at the office. We'll be leaving soon for the station.'

'Great! I need some toy boats – ones that float in the bath. You'll pass that toy shop on the way to the station. Buy every boat you can find.'

Grant chuckled. 'What are you concocting?'

'Nothing you need to know about, and if Freddie and Amelie ask what's going on say you've bought them for your nephew. Please drop the boats off at the tea room as soon as you get here, and I'll sort the rest. Love you. See you later!'

Fifi headed into the kitchen – she'd noticed a raft of rechargeable tealights in the pantry. She plugged them in and crossed her fingers for a successful proposal tonight.

*

At four o'clock, Grant, Freddie and Amelie staggered into the tea room armed with carrier bags. Fifi threw her arms around Grant then hugged her friends. 'It's so good to see you all. I only left London at the weekend, but it seems like ages since we were all together.'

Freddie held a carrier bag in the air. 'What would you like us to do with these? They're for Grant's nephew. He must have a huge bath.'

Amelie chuckled, and Freddie placed his arm around her. Fifi and Grant were up to something, but they couldn't work out what. Amelie took in the sight of the renovated tea room. 'This is so different from the last time we were in here. It's amazing.'

Fifi slid the bags under a table – out of sight out of mind. 'Well, I don't wish to be rude, but I have work to do. Why don't we all catch up at around seven-thirty? I'll meet you in Archie's Alehouse when I'm done.'

Freddie smiled. 'The fireworks don't start until eight. Can't we hide out in the tea room until then so that my parents get a big surprise?'

Fifi spluttered. 'Aren't you popping up to Featherlow Manor to get changed?'

'No. Do we need to?'

Fifi had to think quickly. There was only an hour before closing. The tea room was empty due to tonight's much-anticipated festivities and, she had to admit, she needed help with Sam's secret mission. There must be at least fifty boats in those carrier bags. How was she going to launch all of them with the rechargeable tealights on her own? Jules had finished at lunchtime and left her with just two kitchen hands. Fifi took a risk. 'Well then, I'm going to close early. I'll let the staff go and hide you all in here until later.'

*

Loretta blow-dried her mother's hair. Sam had suggested she get it done and the hairdresser in town was fully-booked for tonight. Eleanor was on edge. 'You don't think Sam's going to propose to me, do you?'

Loretta squealed with delight. 'Oh, that would be wonderful!'

Eleanor shifted in her seat. 'I can't think of anything worse. If he'd wanted to do that, then he should have done it years ago. I'm too old to get married now. I'm happy being Eleanor Dorrit for the rest of my days. I don't want to take Sam's name; Eleanor Comfrey doesn't suit me. You're Loretta Lorne and your brother's Jules Peridot. I like our quirky family structure. I hope Sam doesn't do anything to spoil things.'

22

A FLOTILLA OF BOATS

By seven o'clock, the toy boats were all fitted with rechargeable tea lights. Fifi pressed a button on a remote control and the boats lit up. Amelie clapped her hands. 'You're so clever, Fifi! How far up the embankment will we need to go to launch them?'

Fifi pulled at her short blonde hair then checked the clock on the wall. 'They need to float under the bridge, so it will depend on which way the tide's going.'

Freddie chuckled. 'There's no need to worry about the tide. The river runs downhill. As we look out of the window, it runs from right to left towards the woods. You should reserve the first table on the left of the bridge for Sam and Eleanor. I suggest that Grant and I nip over the bridge with the boats and launch them from the other side. People won't venture over there;

it'll be too dark.'

Grant checked his watch. 'We'd best get moving then before we're spotted.'

Freddie pulled on a beanie hat, and Grant turned up his collar. They grabbed the bulging bags and crept out of the shop and across the bridge.

Amelie giggled. 'This is so exciting. I can't wait for us all to be living here for good.'

Fifi hugged her friend. 'I know!'

The door to the tea room opened, and Loretta stepped inside. 'I'm so pleased you're still here; I have an awful feeling about tonight. There's a good chance Sam's going to propose to my mother and, if he does, he'll break up our family.'

Fifi's eyes locked with Amelie's as she helped Loretta to a chair. 'Take a seat. There's a bottle of prosecco in the fridge; goodness knows who put it in there, we don't have a licence. But we're not open now, so I can't see a problem if I open it.'

Fifi headed for the kitchen, and Amelie sat down next to Loretta, who's eyes widened in recognition of the woman with short sandy hair and sparkling turquoise eyes. 'Oh, my goodness! You're Freddie's bride, aren't you? I didn't know you were back in the village. Is Freddie here too?'

Amelie smiled. 'I'm old friends with Fifi; I was keen to know how she's getting on with the tea room.'

Loretta was in awe. 'Really? How lovely you two have the chance to catch up. I hear you've been on an extended honeymoon this year on Lord Featherlow's yacht. Where have you been, and are you planning to move to Featherlow Bottom any time soon? The residents would love to have Freddie back home, and you too, of course.'

Fifi poured the prosecco as Amelie reminisced about her recent travels. 'We've been so lucky with Freddie's father buying that yacht. We've flown out to the Mediterranean on several occasions to join him: Greece, Spain, Italy. In a way, we've felt a bit sorry for him being on the yacht on his own. He's got a crew, of course, but Annabelle's been too busy with the tea room to join him.'

Loretta sipped her prosecco and smiled. 'Well, I'm pleased Lady Featherlow focused on the tea room, we needed her here in the village. You wouldn't believe what's gone on this year.'

Fifi gulped her glass of prosecco and poured another before sitting down. 'Tell me everything. As the new manager of the tea room, I need to know.' Loretta and Amelie laughed; it was good to have a girly chat.

At seven-forty, the tea room door flew open to the sight of Freddie and Grant. Freddie pulled off his beanie hat. 'We launched the boats, but you're not outside with the remote.'

Loretta stared at Fifi and Amelie whose cheeks were flushing from more than a glass or two of prosecco. They jumped up and Fifi grabbed the remote. 'We're on the case! Just leave it with us.'

Loretta ran after the two crazy women. 'Is there anything I can do to help?'

No-one was sitting at the "reserved" table. Fifi's heart sank, she'd been given one job to do, and she'd failed miserably. Sam and Eleanor were nowhere in sight. The boats could be anywhere by now. Fifi pressed the remote control, and nothing happened. There was one comforting thought; Loretta was concerned about Sam's proposal breaking up their family. Maybe Fifi's failure to help Sam wasn't such a bad thing. Everything happened for a reason.

The girls escaped to Archie's Alehouse. Fifi sat on a bench with her head in her hands. 'What am I like? I had one job to do, and it went miserably wrong.'

Loretta sniggered. 'What was that?'

Fifi tapped a finger to her nose. 'It was secret.'

Amelie smiled. 'You have nothing to worry about

now, Loretta. Sam won't propose to your mother and your family will remain intact.'

Loretta was intrigued. 'Why's that?'

Before Amelie could answer, the first rocket shot into the sky followed by a loud bang and a cascade of shimmering lights. Archie made an announcement: 'The fireworks have started! Everyone outside.'

Lady Featherlow stood on the embankment in awe. She chatted to the residents surrounding her. 'I can't believe that Winston puts on such a good display each year. He loves fireworks. When Freddie was a young boy, it was his favourite night of the year.' She felt a tap on her shoulder.

'Hello, Mother.'

Annabelle turned round to the sight of Freddie. She threw her hands to her mouth, and tears welled in her eyes. 'Freddie! Why didn't you tell us you were coming?'

Freddie embraced his mother. 'I didn't want to spoil the surprise.'

When the fireworks finished, Fifi, Amelie, and Loretta linked arms. Fifi held the remote control. 'Now, we need to find those boats. Freddie said they would sail towards the woods; the river runs that way, and it never changes direction.'

Amelie and Loretta laughed. Fifi kept pressing the remote. 'I'm serious now; we need to find the boats, or I'll get fired. I've used the rechargeable tealights from the tea room. I need to take them back.'

It was spooky walking through the woods late at night with just Amelie's phone light to lead the way. Before long, the girls heard voices: 'You've been the love of my life since I met you. I want us to spend the rest of our days together. Will you be my girlfriend?'

The girls stopped in their tracks, and Loretta whispered. 'He's not proposing.'

They waited with bated breath until they heard: 'I've always been your girlfriend; I'm too set in my ways now to be anything else.'

Fifi jumped up and down and, in the process, pressed the remote control. All of a sudden, the grass surrounding the boat-house became illuminated with twinkling boats. Eleanor gasped, and Sam scanned the woods to the sight of the threesome, who were no longer totally in the dark. He scratched his head. 'There's magic in these woods. I just knew it. How did all these boats get here? How did they light up?'

Fifi held the remote control aloft, and Sam rubbed his chin. He stared at the girls. 'If you stay around for long enough, you'll see them.'

Fifi held her hand to her chest; her eyes were on

stalks. 'Who?'

'The life-size fairies that come out at night.'

Fifi screamed, and Amelie and Loretta linked arms with her. The remote control dropped to the floor as the girls ran back to the alehouse.

Eleanor slapped Sam's arm whilst chuckling. 'You are so naughty. The girls are terrified.'

Sam shrugged his shoulders. 'It'll serve Fifi right. I gave her one job to do, and she messed it up. She didn't even turn the lights on at the start. It's a good job I'm on the ball. If I hadn't spotted the first boats coming through, we'd never have got back here in time to get my fishing nets. They're nice boats. Far too good to disappear out to sea.'

23

SECRETS OF THE WOODS

Freddie and Grant were in the alehouse with Lord and Lady Featherlow when the girls entered. Annabelle patted the bench seat beside her. 'Come and sit down, you three. Winston and I have been advised of Sam's surprise that went slightly wrong. Did you manage to salvage things for him? Has he proposed to Eleanor?'

Fifi blushed. 'I'm so sorry, Lady Featherlow. You can fire me if you wish. I used the rechargeable tealights I found in the tea room to help with my mission for Sam. Unfortunately, I didn't complete the task I was set, and the fairies took over. I'm not going back into those woods again to retrieve them now. You must take the cost out of my wages so you can buy some new ones.'

There were chuckles around the table. Grant

laughed the loudest. 'Fairies in the woods! What makes you say that?'

'Sam told us. You have to see it for yourselves. The boats have all turned up on the grass outside the boathouse. Sam says the fairies are life-size.'

Lord Featherlow squeezed his son's knee under the table – before doing his best to keep a straight face. 'They've turned up again! My mother used to ramble on about the fairies in the woods.'

Lady Featherlow kicked her husband under the table. 'Your mother rambled on about most things, Winston. It's a load of nonsense. Stop frightening the girls.'

Freddie couldn't resist thickening the plot. 'Clara told me loads of stories about the fairies in the woods when she was my nanny. Three fairies, in particular, were very naughty. One was blonde, another was brunette, and the naughtiest one had sandy-coloured hair. Now let me think, what were they called? Yes, that's it! The Blossoms: Apple, Cherry, and Orange.'

Grant sniggered, and Loretta leant forward on the table. 'It's no laughing matter. If you don't believe in fairies, then they will show themselves to you. They only send the bad fairies to sort out the non-believers. Poor Mrs Pankhurst lived to tell the tale – but only just.'

Annabelle gasped. 'I remember that name from years ago. Oh, my goodness!'

Loretta stood up. 'I left my bag in the tea room, would someone be able to unlock it for me? I should head off home soon.'

Amelie stood up too. 'Come along, Fifi. I'll come with you, so you're safe walking back here in the dark. You've had a bit of a shock.'

Once the girls were outside, they burst out laughing. Amelie hugged Loretta. 'I can't believe you came up with that story. No-one believed Freddie, but everyone believed you.'

Loretta giggled, and Fifi gave her a high-five. 'Those men think we're stupid. Do you think I've got away with losing the tea room rechargeable tealights? I'm more than happy to pay for them.'

Amelie smiled. 'Stop worrying about the tealights. Annabelle won't be giving you the sack. I'd love to know how the boats all turned up at the boat-house, though, it was a lovely "non-proposal" in the end.'

Loretta grinned. 'Wasn't it just? My family remains intact. Well, for the foreseeable future at least.'

Fifi unlocked the tea room, to the sight of the prosecco bottle and glasses on the table. 'There's just a dribble left. Let's sit down and finish it off.'

Fifi glanced sideways at Loretta. 'We need to find you a man. I'm an excellent matchmaker. What about Ivan in the alehouse?'

Loretta screwed up her nose. 'He's not my type.'

Amelie leant forward. 'What is your type? I can help too.'

The girls jumped as Jules emerged from the kitchen with flour in his hair. 'Enough of that. My parents have only just "tied the knot" so to speak. I don't want my sister going around with her head in the clouds too. Well, not just yet anyway.'

Loretta smiled. 'How did you find out?'

'Trixie overheard my father's conversation with Fifi this morning.'

Fifi giggled. 'What are you doing in the kitchen at this time of night? Why have you got flour in your hair?'

Jules wiped his hands on an apron before viewing his reflection in a mirror. 'Because you let the staff leave early. They hadn't finished what I'd asked them to do.'

Fifi turned a bright shade of pink. 'Am I in trouble? I'm really sorry about the tealights.'

'What tealights?'

Loretta stood up. 'It's a long story. Is there anything we can help you with?'

Jules's eyes twinkled. 'There certainly is. Come with me into the kitchen.'

*

Sam and Eleanor sat in deckchairs outside the boathouse, looking up at the stars through a clearing in the trees. Eleanor tucked a blanket around their legs, and Sam played with the remote control. It was amazing! Not only did it turn the lights on and off, but it also changed their colours. Eleanor preferred the multi-coloured twinkling setting the best. She sighed, 'I've had such a wonderful evening, Sam. After so many years drifting around the country, I've finally found a place to call home.'

Sam put down the remote control and held his girlfriend's hand. 'Can you believe we have a son called "Jules Peridot"? That was very creative thinking of Clara to ask him to use that name.'

Eleanor raised her eyes to the sky. 'I'm surprised he went along with it. Does he do anything strangers ask of him?'

Sam sat forward in his deckchair. 'I said the same thing to him when I found out.'

Eleanor smiled. 'Well, we are his parents. We'll both

be trying to protect him.'

Sam leant in to kiss Eleanor but was distracted by a twinkling in the woods. 'Crikey! I've been cursed. I should never have made fun of the fairies.'

The sound of music preceded the procession. A rendition of "Somewhere Over the Rainbow" sounded softly before becoming more pronounced. Eleanor clasped a hand to her chest. 'It's our song!'

Sam frowned. 'I've never heard it before.'

Eleanor blushed. 'Well, I told Loretta it was our song. She asked me what it was, and I made something up. All couples have their own song.'

Sam rubbed his chin. 'Really? I'm learning something new every day.'

The twinkling grew nearer, the singing grew louder, and Sam squinted at the sight of Jules carrying a candlelit cake. Not only was his son there, but the residents of Featherlow Bottom had also come out in full force.

Eleanor puffed up her hair and pulled the blanket off their legs before throwing it behind the deckchairs.

Jules was now standing before them. 'I don't know what took you so long, Father, but we couldn't let this occasion go unmissed. We're all delighted that Mother is now officially your girlfriend. Come on, you two, blow the candles out for luck.'

Sam stood up and hugged his son before whispering. 'It's "Sam" remember.'

Jules noticed the tears glistening in his father's eyes. 'I know. I just wanted to get away with calling you "Father" once. That'll do me.'

Sam hugged his son again before walking over to speak to Freddie. 'Since when did you and your friend take up playing with toy boats? I would have thought you were a bit old for that.'

Freddie raised his eyebrows. 'You saw us launching them? We tried so hard to hide in the shadows.'

'I certainly did, not much passes me by. I came home to find my fishing nets to catch them. Eleanor and I had a great time. We've never had so much fun in years.'

Freddie winked. 'So, the life-size fairies didn't help out then?'

Sam chuckled as he shook his head. 'Don't you go telling Fifi that. I need to keep her on her toes if she's managing Lady Featherlow's Tea Room. I pop in there most days. It's a place for people to meet and get a bit of company.' Sam lowered his eyes as he remembered his past; it was also a warm place to go if you didn't have one.

Sam turned round to face his boat-house. It looked magnificent with the colourful twinkling boats surrounding it on the grass. He could see Eleanor and Loretta through one of the port-holes, and Jules was standing outside, chatting to the remaining residents. Sam's heart pounded, and he rushed to the lounge port-hole. He peered inside to the sight of the peridot falcon on the mantlepiece. Phew! He'd left the door unlocked tonight. He wished Eleanor would let him put it back in the oven for safekeeping. Still, relationships were all about compromise. Eleanor was more important to him than a pension fund.

*

Lord and Lady Featherlow walked up the lane to the manor house. It was a cold November evening, but Annabelle didn't notice the chill in the air as she strode along with a spring in her step. Winston increased his pace to keep up with her. The sound of laughter could be heard from ahead. It had been a long time since Freddie's infectious giggles had echoed throughout the woods; what fun they'd had playing hide and seek when Freddie was a young boy. By the sound of it, Fifi and Grant were heading for the manor too – Fifi's laugh trilled through the air. No doubt Annabelle had invited everyone back for an impromptu party. His wife was in her element when Freddie was home.

Annabelle stopped in her tracks. 'Did you hear that?'

Winston chuckled. 'Yes, I did. You've invited all the youngsters back to the manor for a party without mentioning it to me. I'm not silly, you know. I can hear Fifi from a mile off.'

Annabelle gripped her husband's arm. 'I'm not talking about the laughter; I just heard sounds much closer – spooky sounds. Do you remember what happened to Mrs Pankhurst?'

Winston shivered. 'I don't say that I do. We'd best put a step in it; I feel a bit uncomfortable in the dark now. I've never believed in . . . '

Annabelle slapped her gloved hand over her husband's mouth before widening her eyes and winking at him. 'It's a good job we both believe in fairies, isn't it, Winston?'

Lord Featherlow nodded profusely. 'It certainly is, my darling. It certainly is.'

****

Printed in Dunstable, United Kingdom